Advanced Praise for THE SHELTER

"It's *Animal Farm*, in both its optimism and caution, for this generation."
—Ira Rat, author of *Pacifier* and *Participation Trophy*

" *The Shelter* is an allegory for modern society which searches deep between the ideologies of philosophy and the lived realities of its characters. This book is engaging, enlightening, and thoroughly enjoyable."
—S. T. Cartledge, author of *The Orphanarium* and *Cherry Blossom Eyes*

"A revolutionary marvel, Vaughn's *The Shelter* is simultaneously a strong commentary on class struggle, the houseless, and the trauma of being overlooked in modern society as well as an analysis on the philosophical ideas of Diogenes. A story whose universe revolves entirely around dogs with their own invented slang, these animals will show you what it means to be wholly human."
—Andrew J. Stone, author of *All Hail the House Gods*

THE SHELTER

AMY M. VAUGHN

CATLETT, VA

CABAL

AUTHOR'S NOTE

The ancient Greek philosopher Diogenes is widely regarded to have been the first cynic and the first stoic. In this story, everything the character Diogenes says and does is based on actual events in the life of the real Diogenes. His nickname was "the Dog."

PROLOGUE

Jack, a Great Dane, sat in the crosswalk. The elbows of his stiff Army field coat furrowed as he linked arms with the dogs on either side of him. The chain of strays formed a square that blocked the downtown intersection.

The protesting dogs faced inward, looking at each other and not at the angry drivers who would be late for work that morning. Jack took in his comrades' scruffy, serene faces. Even the ones perpetually in motion—plagued by tics or chronically moving their lips as they talked to themselves—were calm. Their twitches and jitters were gone.

They had a purpose. They were playing their part in the Army of Strays. To a dog, they categorically ignored the canine motorists honking their horns and hurling expletives at them. Instead, they rotated their ears like independent satellite dishes, seeking out the signal of their success—the wail of approaching sirens. The more the better. That was their job, the part they were playing in the Uprising of the homeless: they were the decoy.

1

DIOGENES: CYNIC, STOIC, TERRIER

The park downtown was lousy with homeless dogs. Jack didn't like going there, but that was where the Do-Gooders were, with their free sandwiches and clean water and sometimes even toothbrushes.

The only thing more depressing to Jack than being a stray was being around other strays. There were so many these days, so many hard-luck stories, so many ways to fall through the cracks: prison release with nowhere to go, con jobs that wiped out bank balances, being gay or trans in the wrong family, being unemployed or unemployable for too long, abuse, mental illness, addiction.

Not all strays had drug problems, but too many of them did; either they couldn't get the drugs they needed or they took any drug they could find. Jack didn't blame them, the dogs who did whatever came their way. Being homeless was the most stressful spot he'd ever been in, and he spent four years in the war. Homelessness, though, was a totally different kind of stress—not a one-shot adrenaline rush but a long slow burn of uncertainty, of feeling lost and useless and alone. If a dog couldn't handle that without drugs, Jack wasn't going to give them dirt for it.

Even so, that didn't mean he wanted to be around them.

But Jack was hungry, so he walked to the park. At least it was a nice day for a walk. It was early October, when the oppressive city heat finally broke and the pavement no longer singed his hind paws. But the change in weather also meant the chronically homeless who had gone north for the summer were hitchhiking and hopping trains to come south for the winter. The annual migration easily doubled Black Hill's stray population and made Jack all the more wary about how crowded the park would be.

When he got there, it wasn't pretty. It wasn't a spread-out-a-blanket-and-have-a-picnic kind of park in the first place. It was more of a scorched-earth-blending-into-scabby-patches-of-brown-grass kind of park. Off to one side was a collection of rust-crusted playground equipment, and there were concrete benches scattered around, each with metal "arm rests" meant to keep a dog from lying down and having a decent snooze.

For Jack, this underlying beauty was in no way enhanced by the mob of canine life spread across it. There were easily a hundred mutts in that one square block. Mixes of all kinds: Heeler and Shepherd and Hound; Pointer and Husky; Chihuahua and Schnauzer. A good half were Pit Bulls—Pit mixed with Retriever or Rottweiler or Bulldog or just about any damn thing.

Breed didn't matter to Jack. He looked like he was one hundred percent Great Dane, not least because his father had insisted on cropping his ears, but there were no papers to prove any pedigree. And after everything he'd been through, he felt more akin to the mongrels, mutts, and bastards than the purebreds. Anyone on this side of town would tell you purebred was just a euphemism for inbred anyway.

Jack made his way to the line for the pop-up soup kitchen. A few yards away, a group of dogs sat at attention, listening to a gray wire-haired Terrier who was standing on one of the concrete benches. At first Jack thought it was the dirtiest mutt he'd ever seen. But after getting his cup of soup and moving closer, he saw the old dog was just unkempt. His coat was in dreads but not mangy. His eyes disappeared behind untrimmed eyebrows.

"Ownership," the little dog said with gusto, "is an illusion. No one can actually *own* anything; the best they can do is prevent other dogs from using the things they call theirs."

Jack sat down to listen.

"Look," the Terrier went on, "everything that exists is made of the same stuff. Think big—everything in the Universe, every star and planet since the Big Bang—it's all the same stuff. But when people think small they get it mixed up. Somehow they think this cup or this blanket is different: it's mine. But it isn't different. It can't be. The concept of ownership is a rock in a drowning dog's pocket. It's the stuffed rabbit at the Greyhound track. Stop believing in it and you'll be that much closer to freedom."

"Hey Diogenes," one of the mutts barked out, "if nothing belongs to anybody, nothing can be stolen, right?" The heckler looked around for acknowledgement, maybe even a laugh. "Am I right?"

"There can still be theft, knucklehead. However, while a dog can steal from another dog, that other dog will not have lost anything that belonged to him."

"Diogenes dog," the mutt said good-naturedly, "you're crazy."

"It's not that I am crazy," Diogenes replied. "It's just that my head is different from yours. Now if you'll excuse me, I'm going to try to beg some food from that rich guy and his family."

The broken-haired Terrier hopped off the bench and trotted to the corner of the park where several political campaign signs were posted for the benefit of passing cars. He took up a position in front of an especially large placard with a full color picture of a handsome Akita and his family, and he lifted his paws in supplication.

Jack turned to the tricolor Boxer mix next to him. "Who is that guy?"

"That's Diogenes. He doesn't usually talk that long. Sometimes he only says one sentence, but it'll be a doozy. One time he didn't say anything at all, just did his dirt on the bench with everybody watching. Said it was *symbolic*."

"Is he here every day?"

"Most of 'em, and I'll tell you, he's why I'm here. Dirt he says, makes it better somehow."

"I'm Jack."

"I'm Stig," said the Boxer.

The two dogs talked through the afternoon, both appreciative to have some way to fill the time. Stig, it turned out, was a family dog without a family.

"She was my best friend for as long as I can remember, and then she was my wife. All she ever wanted was puppies. We were going to have litter after litter, but instead she got cancer. After the hospital bills and all the lost time at work, by the time she died there was nothing left."

Jack wasn't usually one to open up, but after a hearing a story like that he felt moved to reciprocate. Still, he paused. He wasn't ready, and Stig caught on.

"How about that little mongrel, that Diogenes?" he said, coming to Jack's rescue.

They talked about what Diogenes had said about ownership, and Stig filled Jack in on some of the Terrier's other ideas: things like embracing homelessness as a type of freedom and how, because everything's made of the same stuff, no dog is any better or worse than the next. All dogs are equal.

Sooner than Jack expected, the sun was going down and it was time for them to head their separate ways, Stig toward his truck, which he moved every night and slept underneath, and Jack toward the relative safety of an abandoned warehouse he'd found.

As Jack made his way out of downtown, through neighborhoods, and toward the industrial area by the highway, his head percolating with the new ideas of the day. He wasn't sure if he thought Diogenes was crazy or a genius, but he knew he was coming back tomorrow.

The next day, back at the park, there were already a dozen or so dogs gathered to hear what the wizened cur had to say. Jack recognized most of them from the day before.

When Diogenes got there, moseying in his own time, he hopped on the bench and said just one sentence: "They have the most who are content with the least." Then he hopped back down again.

Most of the onlookers tilted their heads to one side, whether in bafflement or disappointment was hard to say. But as it became clear Diogenes was finished and would say no more that day, they wandered away to chew, swallow, regurgitate, and chew again this heavy (and possibly ironic, if they were paying attention) blade of truth. But Jack stayed and approached the feisty Terrier.

"I've got a sandwich," he said. "You want half?"

They settled into their handout and began to talk in earnest.

"I hear what you're saying about material goods not being the end-all-be-all, but have you looked around? I mean, the way some dogs have so rutting much and we're here with nothing?" Jack's voice slipped into a snarl, exposing the anger that frothed just beneath the surface. "It isn't fair."

"Nothing is," Diogenes said, unperturbed. "The world is a fluke of physics and chemistry. The social system we live under is an arbitrary structure based on power and influence."

"Doesn't that *bother* you?" Jack asked, riled at Diogenes' complacency.

"When I let it. Look son," the scraggly little Terrier told the statuesque Great Dane, "the only truth that matters is this: the less you want and the more you inure yourself to hardship, the easier your life will be. Now stop talking to me, I'm eating."

2

DESTINY'S PHONE

Him: *Send me a pic*

This is how he terrorized her.

Him: *What r u doing?*

Her: *At the store*

Him: *Send me a pic*

He already knew where she was. She knew he knew. He tracked her through her phone. And worse. He'd cloned her phone. Everything she swiped, everything she typed, he watched on his monitor at work.

She would send a pic. She'd take a selfie with a box of biscuits, full view of the aisle behind her to prove where she was. If you asked her why she did it she'd say, "He just wants to make sure I'm safe. The world is a dangerous place." Scratch the surface once and you'd find, "Because being with him is better than being alone.

The world is a dangerous place." Scratch twice, "Because he pays for the phone. He pays for everything." But what she would never ever say, no matter how many times you scratched at her façade, was that she sent the pic because the consequences of not sending it weren't worth it.

Him: *Hey babe. Hows ur day?*

Her: *Good*

Him: *What r u doing?*

Her: *Getting my nails done*

Him: *Send me a pic*

And if she was driving? If she waited until she was done paying for something?

Him: *Where were u?*

Her: *Sorry babe. My paws were full*

Him: *Full of some losers cock. Who were u jacking off this time?*

Or

Her: *I was busy*

Him: *U were busy rutting. Who were you rutting?*

Or

Her: *I was driving*

Him: *To ur rutbuddys house. Who are u rutting?*

Her: *I was not. Why would you say that?*

Him: *Rutting slut*

And that night would be an awful mess of fear and tears, silence and yelling, open- and closed-paw blows, scrambling on the floor. Maybe the cops this time? But she had nothing besides him. No income. No job history to speak of. Nothing to fall back on.

The next day he would find her bruises, hidden under her fluffy white fur. He would kiss them and call them "sugar spots" because they made her sweeter.

3

THE CATTLE DOG'S JACKET

Jack was walking again. Like most strays, he walked so much that the skin on his paws was thick, like the rubber on a basketball thick. Jack walked in part to get to the park downtown and in part because it was better than sitting still.

The way Jack saw it, the homeless had three choices when it came to sitting. First, in the warehouse district—where some of them slept in ones and twos, where cops didn't harass them unless they had been called to a specific building—they could sit on concrete with their backs against metal siding. Not comfortable, but relatively safe. And quiet, which is why Jack chose to spend most of his time there.

Second, in Black Hill's abandoned lots and open spaces, packs of strays set up camps where they sat in the dirt or on pilfered crates and broken chairs. It was a popular option. Being in a community kept the loneliness at bay, kept a dog from going feral. The cops would roust the camps occasionally, when they got around to it, knowing full well that the tents would be set up again somewhere else that night.

And the third place—and worst place—a stray could sit was in public, where they would be scorned or ignored; where maybe one in a hundred Norms would offer eye contact, let alone a smile; and maybe one in five hundred would be a Do-Gooder who wanted to "help." But anything offered beyond a couple of bucks, and the stray would most likely end up getting what the Do-Gooder thought they needed, regardless of what they said they needed. Too much time around the Norms and a homeless dog could come to believe they were invisible, or worse, that they were garbage. Most strays only sat in public when they were desperate and usually in pain. Otherwise, like Jack, they avoided the public gaze like a case of the worms.

It didn't matter where Jack sat; sitting meant remembering, so he walked. He cut through neighborhood streets and alleys when he could, but mostly he loped alongside six-lane thoroughfares. And he tried not to think about anything. He tried not to think about how he was breathing in the pollution that the traffic was breathing out. Or about how it was still better than breathing the swirling dirt of the desert town halfway around the globe where he'd been sent to protect rebuilding efforts. He tried very hard not to think about how he learned that "protecting rebuilding efforts" included hunting down suspected threats to those efforts. About the pop-pop-pop of gunfire and the glass-shattering, metal-twisting crash of exploding vehicles. About being able to see the insides of dogs who a minute before had been friends of his. About the smell of blood on hot sand.

He tried not to think about how coming back wasn't what it should have been, not to think about how he couldn't close his eyes without fear, without reliving experiences no dog should have experienced in the first place. About coming back strung so tight it hurt, hair-trigger overreactive to sounds, to flashes of light, to the looks on other dogs' faces. Coming back to not fitting in any more. Coming back to being abandoned.

In all of this trying not to think, his mind—looking for a soft place to land—came across the little dog and his message about less being better. He was thinking *that* would be okay to think about when he saw a dirty blonde Cattle Dog ahead of him at a bus stop. She was wearing the same kind of field jacket he was.

Jack was a quiet dog. He preferred to keep to himself, but true to his breed, his loyalty was endless toward those he considered part of his pack. When he saw the Cattle Dog's jacket, he wondered if she felt as lost and alone as he did.

Jack watched her dig through the trash and pull out an oversized Styrofoam cup with a plastic lid and a straw. She took the lid off the cup and dumped out the light brown liquid remains of melted ice and someone else's soda. With her back to the busy street, oblivious that her front was to the rest of the world, she fished inside her beige and tan and khaki patterned coat and pulled out a can of beer. She poured it into the cup, chucked the can, and replaced the lid.

"Morning soldier," Jack said as he approached her.

"I ain't no rutting soldier. Not no more," she said back, her words angrier than her demeanor.

"Me neither. I'm just Jack now." Self-deprecation, he knew, went a long way toward offsetting his intimidating stature.

"Then I'm just Phyllis," she said, and she took a deep pull from somebody else's single-use straw.

"You busy Phyllis? Because if you aren't, there's someone I'd like you to meet."

Phyllis took her time answering. She glanced up and down the street. She looked Jack square in the eyes. "Rut it," she said. "My schedule's open."

Jack and Phyllis came upon Diogenes in mid-exchange.

"What happened to you, dog?" one of the many Pit mixes asked. "How'd you get to be this way?"

"What way?" Diogenes asked. "Happy? Content? Honest, willful, strong, genuine, *alive*?"

"Sure, whatever. How'd you get to be so weird?"

"I'll tell you. You remember Erik the Red?"

Everybody knew, or at least knew of, Erik the Red, the old Irish Wolfhound who rarely spoke. He was fur and bones, a living ghost.

"I learned something very important from him," Diogenes said.

"Bullshit. That creepy dude doesn't talk to anyone," the Pit mix said.

"He spoke to me. I asked him *your* very question: 'What happened to you?' I was young and persistent. I spent weeks, maybe months, at the burger joint where he passed his afternoons getting free coffee refills in the same paper cup for days on end."

A few heads in the sparse crowd nodded spontaneously, either because they knew of the Wolfhound's habits or because they had used coffee cups the same way.

"I'd sit with him and hound him. 'What's your deal, Erik the Red? How'd you end up a shell of a dog?' I'd ask him. He was never annoyed. He just sat, staring at me calmly, placidly, you might even say. One day, for reasons unbeknownst to me, he finally decided to speak. Here's what he said: 'The most important thing you can know is what is yours and what is not yours.' And then the old mongrel shut up again. As will I."

And with that Diogenes climbed down from his bench, went to the soup line, and stood backwards in it.

The other dogs murmured as they drifted away. "Fucking loony." "Waste of time." "Still better than watching traffic."

Phyllis turned to Jack. "That guy? You brought me here for that guy? I'm outta here."

"Wait. Come with me," Jack said. She begrudged, and he took her over to Diogenes, who had moved partway up the line now, still facing the wrong way. Every time the line moved, he'd let the dog in front of him go behind him, toward the front of the line, while he stayed where he was.

"Diogenes," Jack said, "This is Phyllis."

Diogenes tilted his head toward the yellow Cattle Dog.

"What did you mean by all that?" she asked. "Knowing the difference between what is yours and what isn't yours?"

"What do you think?"

"I have no idea. I mean, I have nothing. Seriously, I ain't got dirt."

"On the contrary," Diogenes said. "You have the only thing any of us *can* have. You have control over what goes on between your ears. It's the only thing that matters. Everything else can be gone in a flash."

"I don't know. I think having a bed would be nice," Phyllis said.

"It's a trap," Diogenes spat back. "It's cultural indoctrination that chains you to the system. To know your true nature, you have to strip away everything you are not. Comfort only obfuscates, clouds it over. But when you rid yourself of everything you don't really need and live in accord with your true nature, then you will be happy. Free yourself from fate! Get along with as little as possible and nothing can waylay you. You can't lose what you don't have! Count yourself among the fortunate, stray, to have been forgotten by a corrupt system. You've been given freedom!"

The Terrier let the next dog pass him in line.

4

A MESSAGE FROM THE UNIVERSE

When they first met, there had been signs.

Destiny was straightening the lingerie store's rows and rows of panties when she noticed the pack of German Shepherds watching her through the plate-glass storefront. Their kind made her nervous: frat guys in designer casuals, with their leftover popcorn and drinks from Orange Julius that they probably spiked with mini bottles.

They woofed and pointed and leered, taunting one of their own as they did so.

She couldn't hear them because of the music flooding the store, which was at odds with the muzac in the mall commons, but she could imagine: "Come on dog, she's rutting hot. Go talk to her. Don't be such a little bitch."

She ignored them, expecting that the very pinkness of the store would eventually fend them off. It wasn't a bad first job and she needed it. The last thing she wanted to do was lose her cool in front of her coworkers. She was a Poodle, and a white one at that. She couldn't show how anxious she was. That would just feed into the stereotypes.

Here he comes.

Onto the plush pink pile carpet, through the scantily-clad mannequins.

"Hey," he said.

"Can I help you?"

"Yes." His stance was confident, strong. Maybe this wasn't a bad thing. "What time do you get off work?"

On paper, he was perfect. He had pedigree and a lucrative job. He wanted to take care of her, why not let him?

Sure, he could be a dick sometimes, to telemarketers, to wait staff, but "You can't hold his nature again him," her mom said. "Do you want an alpha or just another dog?"

Destiny couldn't shake the feeling he was slumming with her. She could pass for purebred, but she wasn't.

"You need to lock this down," her mom said. "He'll give you the life you deserve."

With dreams of raising little ones, of growing old surrounded by grand- and great-grandpuppies, she married him—only to have him change his tune. He'd never been interested in having litters, he said. "Are you kidding? Any whelps of ours would go straight in the bucket."

She was mortified at first and then disappointed, but she told herself there's a reason for everything. Life could still be full and happy. They had money. They could go out, go to plays, do dinner and a movie, visit friends, travel even.

He didn't want to.

"Would you please stop pestering me with that dirt. I just want to come home to some rutting peace and quiet."

She wondered what lesson she was supposed to be learning. She believed every lifetime served a purpose, taught a dog something. In this lifetime she was meant to learn patience, obedience, humility. At least that was the message she was getting from the Universe.

It was bearable, even with the phone stalking and the occasional bad nights. They only happened once a month, maybe twice, never more than once a week. Certainly not all the time. Enough to keep her on her toes, but not enough to leave. Where would she go? She had no one. She'd become estranged from her mother. He heard her say his name once. "You talking dirt about me? Get off the damn phone." Now he didn't like it when she called her mom.

Still, she could buy anything she wanted, and the house was beautiful, all marble and granite and glass, high fenced with motion sensing lights and alarms—secure.

Of course she daydreamed about walking away. Leaving her phone behind, walking out the front door and down the street. She'd go to her mom's house. Her mom would take her in. Even after the long silence, her mom would understand. She'd do it one day. Not today, but one day. She was sure of it.

Until the day he came home from work, swung his coat and satchel on the wrought iron and glass kitchen table, and told her, "Your mom is dead."

Just like that.

"Your mom is dead. I intercepted the message from the hospital for you."

She didn't know he could do that.

"I did it for you," he said. "I didn't want you to be upset. I told them to bill us for the cremation but we didn't want her ashes."

Just like that, her escape hatch was gone.

5

EMPTY POCKETS, SOUND MIND

Over the next few weeks, Jack would get together with Phyllis and Stig to talk about Diogenes' ideas. One thing they had plenty of was time to talk.

Stig agreed blindly and wholeheartedly with the rabble-rouser. Phyllis thought Diogenes was off his rocker, living in a dream world, which is not to say she disagreed with him, just that she doubted his ideas would bring about any real change. And Jack listened carefully.

They would go together to listen to Diogenes, meeting other dogs who also took him seriously, or were at least intrigued or entertained by him.

"You have to avoid the traps!" Diogenes said. "The job, the family, the HOA, the HMO, the IRS—they will swallow you whole! And you don't need them. You only need three things:

something to eat, somewhere to be, and the freedom to come and go as you please. Never let anyone add to that list of needs. Free yourself from the need to need!"

Another day he showed up with a list written on a scrap of paper bag.

"*This* is the opposite of a shopping list. *This* is a list of things to stop wanting. Ready?"

The dogs who came to listen to him were becoming more regular and more dedicated. A short-haired Collie fished in her pocket and pulled out a pen and a folded piece of paper.

"What are you doing?" Diogenes asked her.

"Taking notes?"

"No! Don't do that. Then you will remember my words and not the ideas behind them. Just listen."

The Collie returned the paper to her pocket.

"If your paws aren't in your pockets, your pockets should be empty," Diogenes said. "Everything that goes into pockets strengthens the system's control over you: cash, credit cards, phones, keys. The content of a dog's pockets is a record of how removed they are from reality. Empty pockets, sound mind."

"Diogenes," Jack spoke up, "what about the list?"

"Right." Diogenes shook his paper in front of him. "Things to stop caring about: money, status, relationships, education, politics, and pleasure. Cast these aside and you will be free!"

"What do you mean free?" asked a grumpy-looking mostly Chow Chow. "We'll be free to die cold, hungry, and alone."

"No! Look around you. There's more than enough effluvia from this society for us to live off of. It only matters that you no longer care that you're living off of what others throw away. It will take courage, of course, to go against the grain. There may even be pain and suffering, but that will only make you stronger!"

One afternoon Stig, meaning well, asked Diogenes, "Don't you want to be taken seriously? If you would trim your eyebrows and not be so bitter all the time—stop acting crazy—you could really make a difference."

"I should clean up my act, then," Diogenes said, "and even more numbskulls will listen to me? Oh, I never thought of that. Maybe I'll put on a tie and write a book. Do a lecture tour? Get popular and make some cash while I'm at it? You must be as dumb as you look. Popularity is a sure sign of emptiness and ignorance. If I prettied up the message, it wouldn't be the ugly truth. Anyway, the Norms are too stupid to turn en masse toward the truth. It's too stark for them; it'd be like touching a live wire."

Diogenes' cantankerousness didn't put them off. Jack, Stig, and Phyllis continued to meet, and more dogs joined their discussions. In between winnowing Diogenes' diatribes down to shorter statements that were easier to understand and remember, they bonded over the hardships of being homeless, the fear and anger that connected them.

Another day Jack caught up with Diogenes, who was perambulating the crowded park, shining a flashlight around in the noontime sun saying he was looking for a real dog. Jack asked him, "If we're all idiots, why do you lecture us? Why waste your time?"

"Because there is only now! Wait, I'll talk really slowly so you can follow me. We only know what we perceive through our senses, right?"

Jack nodded his head.

"Because of that, we cannot prove there is a past or a future. We only know for sure that there's *right now*. Still with me?"

Jack nodded again. He'd heard this before.

"That's the first part. Here's what follows: if the past and the future are illusions and only now exists, we must live each moment as if it were the only moment. Next, if we agree that we ought to speak the truth—can we agree to that? Good. If we agree that we ought to speak the truth, and if I am able to see that there is a better way to live than under the current constricting and unnatural system, I have only now to speak that truth.

"Therefore," Diogenes spoke faster now, swept up in his enthusiasm for his argument, "the stakes are very high and the demand for courage is even higher! Those who know better must be examples of the necessary and radical corrections that need to be made so that canines can live genuine, happy, contented lives!"

Slowing down again he went on, "That's why I try to teach you dim bulbs, as unlikely as it may be that you will understand. Even then I gain. The experience of failure strengthens my indifference."

Jack had always been slow to make up his mind about things. But once it was made up, it was impossible to sway him. He wasn't so sure about Diogenes' skeptical view of his fellow dogs, but antimaterialism was something he could get behind, not least because it made him feel better about his own lot in life.

Later that week, Diogenes showed up with half of his head shaved and a black eye that altered the topography of his face. He walked slowly, curled in on himself, but his expression remained impassive. While Jack thought suffering abuse was unfortunate, and many other dogs fawned over Diogenes because of it—"What happened?" "They *shaved* you?" "No, no, I did that myself."—Jack didn't see Diogenes' injuries as that big of a deal. It wasn't unusual for the homeless to be targets of violence. Often, especially for purebreds, strays weren't even seen as dogs anymore, but as some other, lesser species. Assault and even rape were common. If Diogenes wasn't going to make a fuss about it, neither was Jack.

"Who is happy?" Diogenes asked the motley gathering. "Do you think they are happy—the Norms—in their houses, at their jobs, in their traffic and on their phones? Happiness is not easy to come by. It must be hard won, worked for. Most dogs—nearly ALL dogs—live their lives trapped between misery and boredom. That is their emotional spectrum: misery and sadness and anger on one end, and boredom, ennui, and angst on the other. If they are ever happy, it is only for a brief moment as they swing from misery to boredom or back the other way. A life like that is intolerable, so they seek out distractions to escape their boredom, to escape their misery. But the distractions, whatever they call them—work, drugs, hobbies, violence, creating, collecting—none of them do anything to quell the source of their frustration. Indeed, distractions simply add to their discontent. But *we* are free of those diversions! We can unclutter our minds of distractions! We can unclutter our minds of the constructs that go against our true nature. Strip it all away and become truly self-sufficient. Strip it all away and really live!"

Then Diogenes disappeared. Not in a cloud of smoke or anything so dramatic. He just stopped showing up at the park.

When one afternoon passed without him, Jack didn't think much of it. After two afternoons, he asked around, "Have you seen him?" After three, other strays were worried too.

As word of the eccentric's disappearance spread, the crowd at the park grew. When five days had passed, there were more homeless dogs than ever milling around, talking about him, wondering what happened.

Jack took the lead. "We should be looking for him. He could be hurt worse than he was letting on. We need to search the city."

They split up and checked everywhere they could think of: empty lots and open fields, encampments, abandoned warehouses—anywhere a homeless dog might go to ground. They could not find him.

The next day, the size of the crowd tripled. There was no sign of Diogenes, but several of the new dogs had heard something of his ideas and wanted to know more.

"C'mon Jack, you tell 'em," Stig said.

"I can try," Jack said, and he did his best to explain, in a way everyone could understand, how everything is the same stuff, and what that means about ownership being impossible and every dog being equal. Those who'd been there with Diogenes nodded approval, and the new dogs seemed to take it in.

"Makes sense," Jack heard from one. "I like that," said another.

The next day even more strays showed up, and Phyllis talked to them about the freedom of having nothing, how it was just a matter of changing perspective, of realizing the tyranny of the system. She put it in terms they could relate to.

"We were raised to think success was a job, a family, a home, a car, all the newest technology. And because we don't have that, we feel worthless, like we're failures, like we're somehow incomplete. But we're not worth less than anyone else. Those *things* do not define a dog's true nature. They just cover it up with needless distractions and expectations. If anything, you and me, we live a truer life than the Norms do, with all the made up demands they have to meet every day. They are in chains. We are free!"

By the end of her speech the park buzzed with unharnessed energy.

The next day it was Stig's turn, and he had a plan to talk about pockets and how the things in them symbolized a dog's capitulation to the system. Jack agreed it was a very relatable image. But the crowd had grown too large. Too many dogs couldn't hear him. Instead, the three of them—Jack, Stig, and Phyllis—and a few others of Diogenes' original adherents, went out and talked to smaller groups. They told stories about Diogenes and answered questions, putting things in the easiest terms possible, the way they had come to understand them.

"Less is better than more."

"You can't lose what you don't have."

"Let go of the need to need."

"Empty pockets, sane mind."

"Know what is yours and what is not yours."

As the sun was going down, Phyllis and Jack hitched a ride with Stig back to Jack's place, as had become their habit. On the way, they stopped behind a grocery store where they scavenged some only slightly stale bread and a just-past-expiration-date bag of carrots.

When they got to the industrial part of town, Stig parked the truck in a well-lit lot and they walked the last half block to the warehouse, which, from its faded and peeling paint and broken windows high up the sides, looked as if it had been abandoned for years. The side door had no window, just a broken knob and a hole where a deadbolt used to be. The door swung freely if left to its own devices, but Jack had rigged it with wire to hold it closed, and once inside he angled some beveled two-by-fours against it.

They felt their way through the shadowy, cavernous space to the office, where there were a couple of chairs, an old desk, and some metal shelving, all of which were thick with dust. There were also several candle stumps, which Jack had begged off a priest while he was getting kicked out of a church. He lit one so they could see what they were eating.

"Diogenes is gone," Phyllis said. She ripped off a hunk of crusty bread with her teeth.

"He'll be back," Stig said.

Phyllis rolled her eyes, an implied "Get real." Out loud she said, "Either way, we've got something big going on here, and we'd be fools to let it pass us by."

"What do you mean?" Jack asked.

"I mean we should mobilize the crowd. We have a chance to *do something* here. Something big. Didn't Diogenes say we have a responsibility to try to show dogs a better way to live?"

"What can we do?" Stig asked.

"I don't know," Phyllis said, frustrated. "But we can't keep sitting around talking about ideas. We need to take real action."

Jack and Stig didn't know much about Phyllis, except that she'd come from a bad home and had an even worse time of it in the military—more from her own side than from any enemy. They knew that Diogenes' words had freed her from her past, and that she wanted to share that sense of liberation with others. But they were also aware that this was the first time in her life that anyone was listening to her, and that she seemed drawn toward dominance.

Jack confronted her with this idea, "Are you sure you aren't just power tripping?"

For a flash Phyllis' eyes got wide and her upper lip curled, showing the tips of her fangs, but then she relaxed. As fast as it happened, there was still time for it to register with Jack. *She knows I'm not a threat to her*, he thought. *We're pack.*

She deferred, "Fine. You be the leader then. You've got that whole trustworthy, levelheaded thing going for you anyway."

Stig interrupted them, trying to cut the tension. "If only there was a way to use all these new dogs to empty all the Norms' pockets at the same time. You know, empty pockets, sane mind. Squads of pickpockets maybe?"

Phyllis and Jack looked at each other.

"Empty pockets," she said.

"How far are you willing to go?" Jack asked her.

"What do we have to lose?" she asked.

By morning they had a plan.

6

HOME SECURITY

After her mother's death, Destiny stopped doing her nails. She cut the pompon off her tail and wore her fur in dense curls. She stopped eating except when he made her.

"What? This food's good enough for me but not for you?"

And then he installed the smart-home technology.

It started small. He would be at work and the stereo would turn on, music would play, and her phone would buzz.

Him: *Thinking about you*

If he was mad about something from the day before, he would set the thermostat to sweltering. She couldn't turn it off. She didn't have the program on her phone. She didn't know the password. She could open the windows, until he replaced them with ones that were sealed. "Top of the line," he said. "Unbreakable, leak-proof, energy efficient."

He locked her in.

Him: *U have everything u need*

Him: *Too bad for ur rutbuddy*

He turned off the lights everywhere but the kitchen.

Him: *Shouldn't u be making dinner?*

He haunted the house. The TV would change channels mid-show. He knew which room she was in and would flash the lights to say "Hi." Music would turn on, alarmingly, painfully loud, and turn off just as suddenly or stay on for hours, as if he'd forgotten about her.

She stopped sleeping. She was high strung by nature, and her veins coursed with cortisol, with adrenaline. Every noise, every movement seen from the corner of her eye set her further on edge.

The TV shouted a courtroom reality show. Speakers throughout the house blared mariachi music. It was getting colder by the minute. She tried all the doors. She tried texting him.

Her: *I need out to get my hair done*

He had complained she wasn't keeping herself up.

Him: *There's no appointment on your calendar*

The bathroom, the only room without security cameras, became her refuge. She curled in on herself, laying on the scratchy jute bathmat with a blanket pulled tight around her, and wondered if death wouldn't be better than this.

7

THE UPRISING OF THE ARMY OF STRAYS

Step one of the plan was recruitment. To reach as many dogs as possible, the first thing they had to do was bring in the other adherents from before Diogenes' disappearance. Once they had enlisted their inner circle—the Organizers—Jack brought them all together.

"We need everybody," he told them. "Drunk, sober, sane, crazy, old, young: doesn't matter, we need them. We need whole families, and we need dogs who live in their cars. Tell them it's a demonstration, a protest. We're tired of being treated as less than canine!" The newly christened Organizers' hackles raised in agreement. "But more than anything," Jack went on, "we need to find someone who worked for the phone company, someone who's familiar with the city's telecommunications infrastructure. Ask everyone."

Each Organizer took a district, and within days hundreds of dogs with nothing but time had signed on for the cause. In three weeks they were at least a thousand strong, and they were ready. It was just before Thanksgiving, the one day those with more flock to soup kitchens to show how much they care about those with less.

The day before the protest, the top dogs among the Organizers—the Generals in the Army of Strays—hunched over the desk in the warehouse. A Dalmatian unfurled a map of the greater metropolitan area of Black Hill.

"The red dots are the junction boxes," he said, indicating five points on the map that formed an irregular circle around the city. "These X's along the pipelines are where we need to place the charges. Just taking out the boxes would be too easy for them to replace. Damaging the conduit in multiple locations will take a lot longer to repair."

This wasn't news to anyone. They knew the plan, but they hadn't seen the map until today. That was Phyllis' idea. She didn't want anyone getting cold feet and blowing the whistle on them. The conduits they were targeting contained not only telephone lines but also the fiber-optic cables leading into and out of the city. They were about to explode the internet exchange points that connected Black Hill to the rest of the country and the world.

"We're going to empty their pockets," Jack told them.

"This time tomorrow," Phyllis said, "everyone will have a taste of freedom!"

Stig was less enthusiastic. "Tell everyone to be careful. It's going to be chaos and we don't want anyone to get hurt, Norm or stray."

The Organizers received their assignments; five of them were each matched up with a driver and a team of bomb technicians. The rest, including Jack, Phyllis, and Stig, would lead the traffic blockade and citywide demonstration.

None of them got much sleep that night.

Jack knew that for most of Black Hill it was an unassuming Tuesday morning. The Norms would be getting ready for work, feeding their children, and scrolling through their various feeds, blissfully ignorant that the homeless had pooled their resources to make fertilizer bombs. They would be completely unaware of the high-visibility vests the strays had bought with cash panhandled in front of stores and at stoplights. The vests were another one of Phyllis' ideas, and they were important. With them, the Perimeter Teams wouldn't attract attention while they set up caution tape and dug down to the pipelines.

If everything was going the way it should, at 8 a.m., as the Norms backed out of their garages and started down their peaceful neighborhood streets, the Perimeter Teams would be unearthing bright orange conduit.

Jack couldn't see anything beyond the intersection his Interior Team was blocking. All he could do was hold steady and hope for the best. Stig's concern about the safety of the homeless dogs in the impending chaos plagued Jack. The Organizers had done what they could, keeping known threats—the volatile dogs and the ones who otherwise might be a danger to their team or to the Norms—away from each other and under a watchful eye. But tensions were high that morning. Jack's stomach soured as the excitement of doing something important fought with the fear of going against the

Norms and everything they stood for. He knew he wasn't the only one on edge.

Along with unstable strays, jail time was another serious concern. Jack knew a lot of these dogs had been behind bars before and didn't want to go back. Realistically, the city couldn't jail them all. In the winter, Black Hill had more than fifteen hundred homeless, and most of them were lining the city streets right now.

The Norms who sat in the backed-up traffic were surrounded by strays carrying cardboard signs:

> *Let go of the need to need.*
> *You are not what you own.*
> *Less is better than more.*
> *Extract yourself from the system.*
> *If you owe them nothing, they can't control you.*

The drivers and their sparse passengers ducked their heads and buried their gaze in their phones, waiting for the police to come and return things to normal. They had no idea the threat they were under. But Jack knew.

Most of the dogs in the Army of Strays were recruited with the line that they were participating in an act of civil disobedience; that through this act the homed would finally see the homeless as equals; that after this they would be treated better, suffer less. Not everyone had heard the finer details of Diogenes' ideas, or that the goal wasn't more for them but less for everyone.

Jack knew there would be violence. Too many of the strays were too angry. He could only hope that, instead of taking out their aggression on other dogs, they'd funnel it into property damage, which would further the cause.

Yes, there were going to be arrests. Jack hoped hard that he didn't end up in a cage. He didn't know if he could handle that.

Jack's team was one of fifteen Interior Teams, each of which had been assigned an intersection strategically chosen to cause maximum gridlock. And like all those teams, by the time Jack's watch said 8:10, he and his dogs had attracted a crowd. Curious and angry onlookers gathered at the corners. Drivers were out of their cars, barking and snarling at the strays and harrumphing at each other between updating their social media feeds.

A few dogs to Jack's right, someone threw a paper coffee cup that missed its target and splashed on the asphalt. Another Norm yelled, "Move before I make you move!"

The atmosphere was electric. A shift in the breeze might spark it off.

A few uniformed police officers had been moving around, keeping an eye on the scene. The situation was too big for them to contain on their own. Jack knew they were just there to keep things from getting ugly until help arrived.

Because they were downtown, where there were big buildings and bad parking, and because Jack was sitting in the crosswalk facing the intersection, he didn't see the Riot Squad arrive, but he heard the Norms around him saying "Finally" and "Hope they arrest all these mongrels." Pivoting his ears, he picked up "Make way!" and "Coming through!" He heard the cops' heavy boots clomping and their riot gear clanking as they got closer.

The dogs in the Riot Squad wore their darkened visors pulled down, but Jack could tell they were mostly Shepherds and Pinschers,

Mastiffs and Huskies, and some were Pit Bulls—purebred Pit Bulls, much to the indignation of every Pit mix sitting in protest.

As the police drew closer, Jack felt the dogs on either side of him grow tense. Around the square, fur rose on the strays' backs, giving away their fear.

Jack knew fear, and compared to places he'd been, this was nothing.

"Keep your cool everybody. Stay peaceful and the cops will, too," Jack yelled above the din.

The Riot Squad marched between the protestors and the crowd. To the dogs on the higher floors of the surrounding buildings, it would have looked like a black snake encircling the square. Once in position, the police dogs faced away from the strays. The Norms were the aggressors.

Here and there a few higher-ranking officers edged through the line, which quickly sealed behind them. Jack watched them question his troops, and watched his troops point toward him.

A brindled Mastiff officer approached Jack. "Are you in charge here?"

"As much as anyone," he said.

"Well, they say you are. Do you have a permit for this demonstration?"

Jack could tell the officer knew the answer to that already. But any minute now everything was going to change, and the presence of the homeless dogs in the intersection would be both unnecessary and the least of this cop's problems.

"Since when do you need a permit for free speech?" Jack feigned ignorance, stalling for time.

"You don't. But you do need a permit to obstruct traffic."

Jack's watch ticked over to 8:15. He couldn't hear or feel the explosions, but both he and the officer noticed dogs in the crowd looking up from their phones in confusion, holding their phones high above their heads, or talking to each other: "Do you have a signal?" "I can't send a text." "What's going on?"

"All right, officer," Jack said. "We'll just be on our way then. Sounds like something bigger is going on anyway." To his dogs he yelled, "Okay everybody, we're done here." And they unlinked their arms. The members of the Riot Squad were given the signal to let them disperse, and this team of the Army of Strays casually blended in with the growing pandemonium around them.

Jack turned to leave but the Mastiff took him by the arm. "Not you. You're coming with me."

8

BLISTERS

On the day of the Uprising, Destiny's husband had been gone for nearly an hour when she noticed she didn't have wifi on her phone. She checked the laptop and then the router. The internet was down. She tried the door. It opened.

Destiny moved fast. She packed her biggest purse with clothes and what she thought were essential toiletries, and she walked out into the world.

She walked, with violence and chaos all around her, all the way to the crowded and loud police station, where she waited for hours. And when she was finally able to tell someone she wanted to file a report or press charges or whatever it was you're supposed to do when you've been tortured by your husband, all she got was "I'm sorry. You'll have to come back tomorrow—or in a week or two."

After that she walked mile-long blocks through the darkening city, looking for an open hotel. And when she did find one they said, "Cash only." She didn't have cash. Who carries cash?

It occurred to her, though, that even if they could have taken one of her cards, he would have traced it to her.

It was night now, and Destiny was alone and afraid in a city at war with itself. She kept walking south, putting distance between herself and the foothills, the neighborhood she was fleeing. She could feel blisters forming on the flat pads of her paws.

Would he come looking for her? She was more terrified of that than of the occasional band of strays she passed who were looting or lounging around the high-end stores and expensive restaurants that lined the roads on this side of town. For the homeless, she quickened her pace, but for the few cars that drove past, that might have been him, she turned her head and willed herself to be invisible.

"You don't see me. You don't see me."

She hadn't walked this far in a long time, if ever. Her feet hurt, bad. She needed somewhere safe to sit down. A fountain tucked into the courtyard of a two-story shopping center, hidden from the street. Maybe the Universe was looking out for her.

The blisters were worse than she'd thought. Should she pop them to relieve the pressure? But then they would be open to infection.

Destiny sighed and considered the fountain. She was thirsty, and seeing the water made her more so. But it had surely been treated with who-knows-what chemicals, the kind that keep the water clean-looking through dust storms and bird dirt and the rich bitches of Black Hill spontaneously (driving to this particular shopping center, on a clear day, when the sun was just right and) wading in it, smiling just long enough for the selfie.

As Destiny considered this waste of water, and considered that she'd never considered it a waste of water before, a loud crash echoed in the courtyard; she felt it through the concrete. She startled to her feet, her fur on end and ears lifting.

"Oh dirt!" she heard, then laughter. "I dropped the cash register." More laughter.

Three voices, one male and two female. Should she run? Could she run? Was there any fuel left in the tank? It didn't matter. She was frozen to the spot.

"Rut it. Leave it where it is," one of the female voices said. "Get more food."

Destiny chanced a look in their direction. They were coming out of a restaurant; Table Scraps, the sign said. Two of them, a male and a female, looked like Pariahs—street dogs—like they were one genetic sequence removed from coyotes. Destiny couldn't place the third one's breed. Her short fur was oil-slick black. Her form was sleek and muscular.

They saw her.

"Who's this?" the black dog taunted as they got closer, setting their cargo—bags of potatoes and salad greens, a whole ham, a couple of crates of bottled water—down near the fountain and moving in on her. "Nice coat. What are you doing out here? Shouldn't you be inside with your doors locked?"

Destiny kept her eyes on the ground, her ears flattened back against her head.

They circled her. One at a time, jumping up on the edge of the fountain to be above her. Twitching their lips to show their dirty teeth. Growling under their breath.

Suddenly, Destiny didn't care anymore. She'd been running on adrenaline since 8:15 that morning, and it was gone. Her body relaxed. Her eyes relaxed. She lifted her gaze and looked directly into the black dog's deep brown eyes.

"I can't go home and lock the door. I don't have a home. I don't have anything but what you see here. You wanna take what's in my bag? Go ahead. You wanna rip into me? Go ahead."

The Pariahs looked confused. Their eyes darted to the black dog, asking if it was time to pounce, but she signaled them off. Her demeanor softened.

"Hell of a day to become homeless," she said to Destiny. To the others she said, "Get our stuff. We're taking her with us."

The black dog's name was Ruby. She gave Destiny some water and took her to their camp in a nearby dry riverbed. On the way, she noticed Destiny's strange gait. The Poodle was walking on her toes.

"Blisters?" Ruby asked.

Destiny nodded.

"We'll get those taken care of."

The camp had maybe a dozen tents or tarps set up, but most of the sites were empty. Destiny had never been camping in her life, let alone homeless. She wondered what these dogs did all day and how they slept on the hard ground. She wondered where they went to the bathroom and realized that was a strange way of putting it since there was neither a bath nor a room involved.

Ruby led her to a large gray tent that was strung between two trees. Belle and Beau, the near-coyotes, followed with their loot.

"Looks like almost everybody's found other accommodations for the night. Put your stuff in here," Ruby said, holding back the tent flap. "Then we'll see if Pete's around."

Destiny crouched inside the dark tent. She set her purse off to the right of the opening so no one would trip over it. It seemed to hit the floor prematurely, as if the ground inside the tent were raised compared to outside. The sensation was jarring. She brushed it off, eager to have her feet seen to. When she turned around, Belle was shining a flashlight in her face.

"Hellhounds!" Destiny said. Usually a startle like that would have left her heart pounding for half an hour, but this was different; she wasn't scared, she was mad, and it showed in her face.

"Sorry," Belle said. "We just need to put this stuff away." She redirected her light to the floor as Beau humped in a load of goods.

In the glow of the flashlight Destiny could see that the floor was completely covered, every inch, in rolling piles of clothes. As she ducked out of the opening, Destiny's only thought about the expanse of used and dirty clothes was that at least it would be better than sleeping on the ground.

"Pete!" Ruby yelled as she and Destiny walked toward a pristine (for these conditions) blue tent. It was perfectly shaped, while all the other ones sagged or bulged from missing or broken tent poles.

"Pete, I got a girl needs seeing to. If you're in there, tell me we can come in and you're not gonna whack us with that stick."

Something shifted inside the tent. Someone coughed to clear his throat.

"Whadya bring me?"

"Water. We've got water for days. We're coming in."

"No, no. I'll come out. More room, better light. I'll get my kit."

Ruby got a fire going in a pit near Pete's tent. Belle and Beau came back with their flashlights. Pete—a deeply dirty, middle-aged Golden Retriever—sat on the edge of a stack of wooden pallets, and in front of him Destiny had the seat of honor: a plastic folding chair with a crack in the back that would bite her and pull her fur if she tried to lean against it.

Pete tapped his thigh. Destiny hesitated.

"C'mon. I used to be a scout master. Dealt with lots of bad blisters on the trail. None like what I've seen on strays though. I've done this dozens of times, maybe hundreds."

Destiny lifted her paw and set it on Pete's lap.

"You got soft skin," he said.

She jerked her paw back, left it hovering in the air like she was ready to kick him with it.

"No, no. Don't get me wrong. Just been a while since I've seen a paw that wasn't made out of callouses." He reached out his fore paws and she set her hind paw back in his lap.

Pete opened his kit, a clear plastic baggie that held a nearly used-up roll of duct tape, some beat-to-hell packets of antiseptic wipes, a lighter, and a two-inch safety pin. He used one of the wipes on his hands. When he turned his attention back to Destiny's paw, he whistled through his teeth.

"That's a doozy. Dog, that's an odd thing right there."

Destiny wasn't sure if he was talking to her or to Ruby, until he picked up her paw and angled it so Ruby could see better.

"It covers the whole thing. See there, how the dark skin of the pad is cracked and the pink shows through from underneath. I've never seen such a big bubble. It's like they've never been walked on."

All four of them—Pete, Ruby, Belle, and Beau—looked at Destiny for an explanation, eyebrows and ears lifted. She sighed.

"I haven't been out of my house for months. I've been trapped, a stupid rutting prisoner of a stupid rutting alpha. Are we good now? Can we do this thing?"

Belle, Beau, and Pete raced to see who could look away fastest, but Ruby said, "You don't have to say another word about it, sugar."

"Ready?" Pete asked.

Destiny nodded, and Pete ran the tip of the safety pin through the lighter's flame. He positioned her paw between his legs and cleaned the pad with an antiseptic wipe. He had barely pressed the needle-sharp point to the edge of the blister before it disappeared through the skin, and as he withdrew the pin, straw-colored plasma squirted out onto the ground. For a few seconds, the liquid leaked out, then it slowed to a drip. Pete gently kneaded the pad, helping the last of the fluid find its way out. Drained, the skin hung slack, like an empty balloon. He wrapped the paw in four layers of duct tape, giving Destiny a makeshift cast. She didn't like how it felt—there wasn't a dog alive who was comfortable having their paws covered—but she knew she'd like an infection even less.

"Let's see that other one," Pete said.

9

JACK IN JAIL

Jack was doing alright in the city jail, better than he'd thought he would do anyway. He was being kept in a large pen with a dozen other members of the Army of Strays. They had beds and food and time outside. The windows were barred, but there were windows. And he was allowed visitors.

Phyllis had managed to keep a low profile during the Uprising, and the day after the protest, she came to see Jack. It wasn't until her visit that he found out just how successful their plan had been.

She painted the picture for him of all the Norms realizing at once that they couldn't get to the internet, that they had no wifi, no cell signal, and that even the few remaining land lines weren't working. She told him how they turned to their TVs but found only black screens. The occasional old mutt who had an antenna and a digital converter felt pretty smug about their broadcast channels, but everyone else—corded or cord-cut—was in the dark. Most of them ended up in their cars, listening to the radio to find out what was happening.

And when that no-nonsense public radio reporter told them the internet backbone had been damaged? Well, first they had to listen to him explain what an "internet backbone" was, and when they heard how it had been targeted in "several tactically specific locations," that's when the real panic set in.

Black Hill is being invaded by terrorists!

But as the smooth voice continued, and they learned that this well-planned attack wasn't pulled off by terrorists but by the homeless, they went from scared to angry in a flash. They were fuming. And when the radio voice told them, with perfect enunciation, that it would be several days, possibly a week or more, before communication channels could be repaired, then their wheels really started to turn.

The anxious breeds hunkered down in their houses, but most dogs took to the streets.

Cash became the first necessity. Debit and credit cards were worthless. For safety, the banks all closed their doors and dropped their security bars. ATMs were useless; unable to check account balances, they refused to dispense any cash. Grocery stores were overrun and cleared out. Looting was rampant.

Internet-based security systems were offline along with everything else. Even if a store had CCTV, the streets were gridlocked and all the cops were either stuck in traffic or trying to clear it. Packs—and Phyllis didn't know if these were strays or not but she suspected they were—went into neighborhoods, broke into houses, and created enormous bonfires out of people's possessions.

"It was glorious," she told him. "Well, that part of it was."

There was widespread chaos and panic and fear. Everyone who owned a gun had it on them, and several dogs were shot. Half a dozen died.

One of them was Stig.

Jack knew that Stig had been team leader for an intersection in a part of town lined with strip malls. What he didn't know, what Phyllis had to tell him, was that after the tricolor Boxer was certain the internet was down, he told his team, as planned, "We're done here." The next step was supposed to be for them to join the protestors with their signs and their chants, but a few of Stig's dogs broke off on their own. They threw planters through the plate-glass storefronts of the nearest row of businesses: a 99 cent store, a bakery, a Radio Shack. They ate fresh bread and pastries from the bakery while they ransacked the other businesses.

Stig chased after them. "Hey!" he barked, "C'mon guys. Knock it off. This isn't what we're about." But they ignored him. He got closer. "There are cops everywhere around here. You're being idiots." He went into the dollar store, where the protestors-turned-looters were shoving food in their pockets and sweeping their arms across shelves, dumping merchandize to the floor.

Two police officers came running into the parking lot. One of them cupped her paws around her muzzle, forming a makeshift megaphone. "Come out with your paws up," she yelled.

"Okay officers," Stig said, turning around and moving toward the shattered storefront. "We're cooperating. We're unarmed."

But the dog behind him wasn't. The officers drew their weapons. A shot went through Stig from behind. He might have lived if an ambulance could have made it to him.

Jack took the news of Stig's death hard. The family dog without a family had warned them that dogs were going to get hurt, but it had never occurred to Jack not to go forward with the plan.

He tried to be stoic about it. *What would Diogenes say?* I did what I knew to be right in that moment. I can't change the past.

It didn't make him feel any less guilty or sad.

The second day after the Uprising, during Phyllis' visit, she told Jack that almost every business in Black Hill was closed. Only the hospitals and a few owner-operated stores were open. After the gridlock cleared, there was a run on gas stations. Everyone who could afford it hit the road, which choked the highways through the night and into the next morning. Phyllis laughed as she told Jack stories about purebreds having to piss and make dirt on the side of the interstate.

Now, the gas pumps were dry; large sections of downtown and the poorer south side were on fire; and looters and vandals had moved into the foothills to take advantage of the empty houses the purebreds left behind. There were stories, though, that every once in a while they'd come across a well-off survivalist who was ready for them, some old cur living out their zombie apocalypse fantasy. Only these dogs weren't back from the dead, they were just poor. Didn't matter. They were still considered fair game.

When she came on day three, Phyllis told him that every single video and magazine had been looted from every single porn shop.

Most of the Norms—those who hadn't been able to drive away—were completely lost. Without their jobs, their phones, their streaming services, they didn't know what to do with themselves, what to do with all that time. Water and electricity suffered glitches, but still flowed; conditions weren't primitive, but most dogs still felt like they were living rough.

The boredom was profound. Some of the Norms tried to busy themselves with chores or projects or the books they'd been meaning to get to. But daycares and schools were closed, so pups were underfoot, and they were bored too, especially the ones who were used to their own devices.

Teenagers took it the worst. Their phones and games and social media were gone. Their source of self-esteem, their imaginary audience, their reason for living had disappeared. They were the first to become intolerable to be around. Their eyes grew vacant. They would snarl and snap for no reason. Those prone to drooling, as some dogs were, could have been mistaken for rabid. Packs of adolescents were even worse. Being with each other only magnified how moody and angry they were. Many Norms were secretly grateful the Council had implemented a strict dusk curfew.

Neighbors with DVD players or stand-alone gaming systems had the most popular houses on their streets. Dogs did go outside more, talk to each other more, and a lot of yards were taken care of. Some Norms even enjoyed the quieter routine of life out from under the 'net. But for most, the constructive coping didn't last, and right beneath it was anger. Even though they took it out on each other—on their loved ones and roommates and friends— those were poor substitutes for the true targets of their rage: the homeless. It was the homeless who had disrupted their lives, taken away their screens, exposed their addictions. It was the homeless they wanted to punish.

On day four, Phyllis stopped coming to the jail.

10

THE SHELTER

Destiny was in the dry riverbed encampment when the National Guard dogs raided it. She could walk normally by then, but was hesitant to take off the tape. What if it wasn't really healed? What if the tape pulled off the skin? Pete said it was best to wait until the tape fell off by itself, but she was impatient. What she really wanted was to soak her paws to loosen the tape, but there was nowhere nearby to do that.

It turned out not to matter.

Just before dawn on her fourth day as a stray, Destiny was sleeping in the gray tent a few feet away from Ruby. Belle and Beau had moved into one of tents left empty by dogs who were squatting in nicer places. Destiny had tried sleeping in a different tent, one with a piece of foam and a pillow, but she'd stayed awake all night. It was better knowing Ruby was there.

Destiny lay under a thin blanket on the floor of clothes. It didn't smell so bad to her anymore. The first night, the reek of dirt and sweat had made it hard to sleep, but she'd grown used to it; it wasn't much different from her own smell now.

She was startled awake by a high-pitched squeal followed by an amplified voice: "Come out with your paws up. We have you surrounded." They'd heard rumors about the roundup but didn't believe it. They thought they'd have time to move or at least to run. But the Guard was there in force, in their fatigues and helmets, with their rifles and sidearms.

Destiny barely had time to process what was happening before she was boarding the white bus along with Ruby and Pete, Belle and Beau, and a few other stragglers. They were allowed to bring one bag each.

Nobody put up a fight, but quiet curses were said against the Guard dogs and against the Army of Strays that provoked their presence.

Cesar Millan Elementary used to be a K-8 school in south Black Hill. Its closure, due to low test scores, had been vehemently protested by the local community. For the past three years it sat empty.

It was a cute school, with cartoon murals of dogs helping each other in the hallways. It was a place where puppies could feel safe and happy. In its first year, they let the students vote on what the school colors should be, and the kids decided on all of them, so the school's colors were the rainbow.

Like every school, Cesar Millan Elementary was surrounded by a tall chain-link fence. Recently, three rows of barbed wire had been added to the top of it, and the rolling gate that closed off the parking lot had been replaced with a newer, sturdier version. A guardhouse had also been added.

The school was made up of ten buildings, eight of which were long rectangles, with classrooms off either side of a central hallway. There was one of these for each grade, first through eighth. These buildings radiated out around the playground like the petals of a flower or like rays of sunshine in a puppy's drawing. Each one was a different color of the spectrum, from red for the first grade through violet for the seventh. The eighth grade building was all the colors: the Rainbow Building. The kindergarten, an octagon, and the gym/cafeteria, a much larger rectangle, were outside the circle, across the multipurpose field from one another.

The kindergarten was closest to the parking lot. As the bus pulled in, Destiny watched dogs in casual business wear go in and out of the white octagonal building, their professionalism at odds with its murals of puppies playing ball and chase and tug-of-war. A printed sign in a protective plastic sleeve taped to the side of the entrance read "ADMIN."

Destiny and the others on her bus were shown to the Green Building. Red, Orange, and Yellow were already full. In their classroom, the bulletin board said "Great Job Everybody! Have a Safe and Happy Summer!" in cardstock bubble letters. Bright cheery posters about grammar and punctuation lined the walls. The room was crammed full of bunk beds.

Destiny grabbed the bunk above Ruby's, and the two females tried to size up their new roommates. Nearly every other dog was doing the same, though there were a few who sat hunched on their bunks, eyes lowered.

Before long, a business casual came by. "Time for in-processing. Leave your things on your bunks." He led them to the gym, where every dog was forced to strip and shower. They stood in line waiting to be checked for ticks and fleas. Those who had them, which was most of them, were shaved. Destiny breathed a sigh of relief when none were found on her.

She had just been given a white t-shirt and dark blue work pants when she was pulled aside and taken to the clinic.

"What?" she asked. "What's wrong?"

"Wait here," was all she got.

Eventually the veterinarian came in and looked at her hind feet. He ordered the nurse to soak them until the tape came off easily. When it was over, her paws were tender but not ripped or infected.

Later that afternoon the strays were led out to the playground for orientation. A soft, wide chocolate Labrador, whose muzzle was partially white, stood on the top of a slide to speak to that day's newcomers. There were easily fifty of them, maybe more.

"Welcome," he said affably, as if he were not in charge of an internment camp. "My name is Abe and I am Black Hill's newly appointed Dog Catcher."

A groundswell of growls rumbled through the crowd.

"Wait, wait, please." Abe lifted his paws in what could have been either a gesture of submission or an attempt to keep the strays in check. "The title is antiquated. My job is to help you get back on your paws. And the way we're doing that here, you should know, is with a foster care system."

More growling. "The rut is he talking about?" "This is dog dirt." "We have rights." "You can't hold us here."

"Listen! Listen! I understand your complaints, but consider this a welcome alternative to jail, since you've all broken at least one law—the Urban Camping ordinance."

"That's just a fine," someone barked.

"Not since the Uprising. The Council made it a punishable offense," the Dog Catcher said.

"No way." "Dirt eaters." "Those rutters."

"But listen, the new system is already working. Community members are coming in and adopting strays. They're taking them home and sponsoring them, giving them a place to live, food to eat, and a bed or a couch to sleep on. It's a helping paw from the community until you can find work and move into your own place."

"Seriously?" a stray said. "That sounds sketchy as hell."

"Do we get any say in who we go home with?" another yelled out. Then to her neighbor, "I doubt it."

"I know, I know. It's not ideal," Abe said, doing his best to manage the riled-up crowd. "But complaining won't change the fact that our doors open tomorrow at eight a.m. for potential fosters, and that reveille is at six o'clock, so you'll have plenty of time to have breakfast and make yourselves and your rooms presentable."

Sitting down with her tray on the long, low bench of the cafeteria table, Destiny couldn't hide her heartbreak. She'd finally escaped one prison only to go directly into another. What she wouldn't give for a tarot reading, an astrologer, a Magic 8 Ball even, anything at all to help her make sense out of what life was trying to teach her.

"Don't worry, girl," Ruby said. "We're in a beauty pageant now. You'll be out of here in no time."

Destiny knew that ought to make her feel better, but it didn't.

11

THE RAINBOW BUILDING

Jack wasn't doing too well. He was in the Rainbow Building, locked in a classroom by himself. The windows were painted over; there were rectangles on the multicolored walls where someone had taken down posters; and there was a set of bunkbeds, but only one thin, blue and white striped mattress.

Jack had been the Shelter's first occupant, and they hadn't told him anything. He'd been there a few days, he thought—definitely less than a week—and already his mind was starting to collapse in on itself. There was nothing to do in this room but remember.

At first he tried to use movement to stay in the present, but after his muscles cramped from too many pushups and crunches, too much pacing, he had to come up with other ways to focus. He tried to think about his childhood, about movies he knew by heart, about books he'd read, songs, TV shows, commercials, anything. But nothing was strong enough to keep the war away.

He spent hour after hour reliving the most horrific moments of his life. He used to know why this happened to him. At the VA, he'd been given a pamphlet. It used a lot of Latin-sounding words, like cortisol and hippocampus, to explain why his most messed up memories stayed right at the surface, why instead of acting like things that happened in the past, these surface memories tricked his brain into thinking they were happening right now, again and again.

Inside the rainbow-painted room, a roadside bomb took out the lead vehicle in his convoy. He was driving the second Humvee.

The carnage kept happening, right there in Cesar Millan Elementary. It kept happening over and over, spliced with every other memory Jack had of being in the desert.

On a chaotic city street, a sniper shot the soldier next to him through the eye.

In the desert Jack was always on his guard. Anything could happen, any time. On missions—protecting the contractors laying utility pipelines or, worse, combing through towns, rooting out threats—he couldn't trust anyone who wasn't on his team. Every face he saw he smiled at, always an ambassador for his country, knowing that any dog—no matter how old or how young, no matter how friendly looking—any dog might be armed or have a bomb strapped to them.

In a mountain village, an anti-personnel mine buried in the dirt floor of a stone house took one leg each from two of his squad mates.

Jack was at this life-or-death level of on-his-guard for days in the Rainbow Building. He was there so long that his hippocampus was drowning in cortisol. His trauma was causing him trauma. Damage layered on top of damage. The room around him felt unreal. He was dissociating. His brain had gone to DEFCON 1, pulled out the biggest guns—unhitch, jump, pull the cord, float in the warm quiet void.

He could hear them in the hall.

At some point Jack had lost consciousness. How long had he been out? The sun was up again. Probably less than a day.

"Kinda backwards that this was the first building we prepped since it has the fewest strays."

Jack knew that voice. It was the pudgy middle-aged Lab who held the keys. He moved to the door. The window was covered from the outside. He leaned in to press one pointed ear to the glass.

"It'll fill up soon enough," said a satiny feminine voice.

As they got closer, Jack heard nails clicking on the rainbow-tiled hallway. Only rich bitches had long nails. It meant they didn't have to walk much. They painted them bright colors, showed them off to each other. Jack wondered what Diogenes would think about that.

"What will we do then? Didn't you say fosters can't choose from this building?"

"Yes, I did. Once these rooms fill up with recidivists and the non-adoptable, we'll be forced to begin the euthanasia program," the velvet voice said without a hint of remorse. "Didn't you read the ordinance, Dog Catcher? We're going to eliminate homelessness, by any means necessary."

The nails clicked away down the hall. Jack stood up into a cloud of dizziness. He stumbled back until he ran into his bunk. How long did he have?

12

THE COVINGTONS

Ruby was right, Destiny was among the first strays to go home with a foster family.

Her second day in the Shelter, the day after in-processing, Destiny sat on her bed while Do-Gooders perused the rooms. By the time they got to her, they'd already been through the Red, Orange, and Yellow Buildings. Worn down by the pleading eyes and hard-luck stories, the Norms were no longer considering the merits of each dog, but looking for that special something that reminded them of who they wanted to be or of happier times.

The strays didn't have to stay on their beds during Foster Hours, but they did have to stay in their room. At the door was a clipboard with a roster listing each dog's name and predominant breed—unless it was Pit Bull or Rottweiler or some other stereotypically violent line. Those were listed as their next most prevalent genetic type.

The elderly couple—her a large cream-colored Labradoodle with an enormous pocketbook and him a Bearded Collie in glasses and a sport jacket—didn't even look at the dogs in the room before scanning the roster.

"Oh!" she said to him. "A Poodle! What do you think?"

He pushed his glasses up his snout and held the paper close to his face.

"Worth taking a look I suppose," he said, as he lowered the clipboard and scanned the room. "There." He pointed out the white Poodle to his wife.

They walked right to her, ignoring every other dog in the room.

"Hello you pretty thing! I'm Mrs. Covington," the wife said, holding her paw out for a shake.

"And I'm Mr. Covington."

"I'm—" Destiny tried to introduce herself, (needlessly, since they already knew her name from the roster) but before she could get a word in, Mrs. Covington was already saying, "We're going to take you home and give you a whole new start in life. Won't that be wonderful? Come on now, get your things."

Destiny stood with Mrs. Covington in the hallway of the couple's completely average three-bedroom, two-bath suburban home.

"And this," Mrs. Covington said as she opened the bedroom door, "is where you'll be staying." Her face radiated pride.

Destiny looked in, closed her eyes, and looked again. The room, which wasn't very big, was very pink. The walls were a deep pink, a Pepto-Bismol pink, with ornate white molding around the top.

The carpet was bubble gum; the comforter a creamy rose pink with white lace trim around the edges and around the pillow shams. There was a pink desk and a white wooden chair with a pink padded seat. There was a pink dresser with a pink framed mirror that reflected back solid pink.

Rut, Destiny thought.

"It'll be great," Destiny said.

"Of course it will. You just get in there now." Destiny realized she hadn't actually entered the room. She did so slowly, cautiously, as if the pink might stick to her and stretch in long elastic strands when she tried to pull away.

"There you go," Mrs. Covington said. "Now hurry up and get settled. Dinner is in fifteen minutes." She closed the door, leaving Destiny alone in the very pink room.

I can do this, Destiny thought. *It's only temporary. Get a job, a few paychecks. I'll have first and last months' rent. I can do this.*

She didn't unpack her bag. Instead she lay on the bed and closed her eyes. Next thing she knew, Mrs. Covington was yelling through the door. "You're late! I said fifteen minutes."

"Sorry," Destiny said rubbing her eyes and snout with her paws and standing up. "Must have drifted off."

"Well," Mrs. Covington huffed, "food's waiting."

The table was set for a family-style meal, and Destiny sat down into a silent ceremony of plate passing and precise servings meted out by Mrs. Covington. She waited until both of the Covingtons had started eating before picking up her fork.

As they ate, Mr. Covington never looked away from his food, but Mrs. Covington stared at Destiny with wide eyes, as if expecting her to say something. Trying to be polite, to start a conversation, Destiny asked, "Was that your daughter's room?"

"What?!" Mr. Covington snorted, as if she'd accused them of something awful, like keeping dead bodies in the basement or not tipping his caddie.

"Oh no! No, we would never," Mrs. Covington said. "I mean, we're very *progressive*, of course. We were one of the first interbreed couples at our school. But a *litter*? That just wouldn't be fair to the pups." She shook her head in a way that let Destiny know she expected better from her.

"I just thought . . . pink room . . ."

"Yes, well, that," Mrs. Covington set down her fork. "We took in my niece Abigail, my sister's daughter." She looked to either side of her for secret spies and stage whispered, "ADDICTION." Then, with that nastiness behind her, she went on. "But it didn't work out. The girl just wasn't *grateful*. And anyway, she couldn't follow the house rules, so we sent her to live with someone on her father's side. Poor thing, life hasn't been easy for her." Mrs. Covington looked at Mr. Covington. "I wonder how she's doing."

Mr. Covington nodded seriously and continued eating his dinner.

"House rules?" Destiny asked. Discomfort stirred in her belly. Her husband had house rules.

"Nothing to worry about. Just normal things," Mrs. Covington said. "Pick up after yourself. Awake by six a.m. Lights out at nine."

"Keep the noise down!" Mr. Covington chimed in.

"No grooming anywhere but your bathroom. No laughing when you're alone in a room. And ask before you eat anything. I mean, I have to be able to run the household, don't I?"

"And your niece broke the rules?"

"She was just plain willful."

"How old was she?"

"Let's see . . . just starting high school if I remember right."

Poor girl, Destiny thought, but she didn't say anything aloud. She also didn't ask what happened when someone broke a rule. She didn't want to know.

Destiny tried. She really did. She spent weeks filling out applications, turning them in, hoping to hear back from someone, anyone. The process was easier once the internet was back up, but still, no one was biting.

"I was trying to let you do this on your own," Mr. Covington said with an air of being severely put upon. "But what you need is a good resume. Come. I'll help you write it." He hefted himself up from his recliner in front of the television.

They sat at the dining room table with a yellow legal pad between them, and when it came time to list her "Education and Training," Destiny had to admit she'd never been to college or had any training past maintaining the panty bar at Victoria's Secret.

Mr. Covington did nothing to hide his shock and dismay. "Oh, erm, (cough) we assumed that as a Poodle . . ."

Destiny let the conversation hang. Nothing she could say would improve her standing with the Covingtons.

After two months of pink walls and uncomfortable dinners, Destiny landed an interview with a puppy-care center that was forty-five minutes across town by bus.

"Isn't that wonderful!" Mrs. Covington crooned. "What are you going to wear? It has to be young and fun and nothing at all like your regular clothes."

Destiny wasn't sure what she meant. Her clothes weren't any different from what every other bitch her age was wearing, even if she didn't have very many different outfits.

"I'm sure Abigail left something behind that would be perfect. She was big for her age, you know. Took after the Labrador side."

Mrs. Covington dragged Destiny to the pink room. She opened the closet and started digging thought it, her arms windmilling clothes out into the room.

"Here it is! I don't know why she didn't take it with her." "It" was a raglan t-shirt with pink sleeves and a puffy plastic glitter iron-on koala. "Now where's that skirt?"

From the one photograph the Covingtons had of Abigail, and from the raccoon mask make-up she was wearing in it, Destiny figured Abigail was not the glitter koala type, unless it was ironic. And this shirt was not ironic.

"Here you go!" Mrs. Covington emerged from the closet with a high-waisted acid-washed denim miniskirt. "Aren't you going to look so cute!"

Whether it was because of the clothes or despite them, Destiny got the job. From the first day she knew it wasn't going to be easy. She didn't mind cleaning up the little ones' dirt and pee and spit up. It was the sudden loud noises that caused her to freeze, caused her heart to race and her fur to stand on end, and, except during naptime, there were sudden loud noises all the time. Squeals of joy, screams of pain, wails of disappointment, crashes as block towers fell and bins of toys were dumped on the floor, as toy cars and trucks smashed into each other.

Destiny spent the whole day, every day, on edge.

Thank God for naptime. Destiny volunteered to stay with the pups while the other bitches went outside to check their phones or have a smoke or just not be in that room anymore. In the quiet room with the resting puppies, Destiny regained her equilibrium and, even though the startles started back up immediately, without naptime, she wouldn't have lasted as long as she did.

Her first paycheck was disappointing. It was going to take a lot longer than she thought to save enough to move out of the Covingtons' house.

It's okay, she told herself. *At least you're safe. It takes time to build a life.*

She could fake it as long as she kept her attention on the future, but when she started to think about her past or the present, she'd see the pattern: the prison of her husband's house, the prison of the Shelter, the prison of the Covingtons' home. It wore on her, not being in charge of her own life.

And then one day at work, after watching a male Schnauzer pup push over a female Beagle pup because she was taking her turn on the paw-painting board, and watching her coworker give in to the male instead of stand up for the female, Destiny was done. She'd never been comfortable with the biting and the fur-pulling and the yelling and the crying, but this was a step too far.

It wasn't a conscious decision. She simply walked out the door. Returning to the Covingtons' didn't occur to her. She couldn't face that house, those people, that room anymore.

She didn't think about the trouble she'd be in when the Shelter found out she'd disappeared.

She just walked.

13

BRUNO THE BULLDOG RUTS THINGS UP FOR EVERYONE

As the Rainbow Building filled up, Shelter administration buckled to pressure and gave them recreation time, but they also got bars on the windows and armed guards.

It was no secret that potential foster families never toured the Rainbow Building. And there were rumors—rumors Jack knew to be true—that there was only one way out, and that was by way of the Rainbow Bridge.

Jack still had his own room, which was how the guards talked about his solitary confinement. The other Rainbow residents were crammed in, ten mongrels and miscreants to a classroom. It was getting easier to earn a spot in the Rainbow Building. What had started out as an extreme alternative when there was no other way to reform a stray was becoming the go-to answer when a dog got a reputation as a troublemaker. This was especially true if they were ugly or disabled and unlikely to be chosen by a foster family. Not disabled like missing a limb or squinty-eye blind or anything else that made for good social media pics, but the ones who were morbidly obese or schizophrenic or had the mange—nobody was going to take them home.

Once rec time started, it didn't take long for the Rainbow Building dogs to choose sides: were you with Jack or against him?

It was a Bulldog called Bruno, with a pronounced underbite and hash-mark scars around his left eye, who made it his business to get right up in Jack's face while they were out on the playground. He was the kind of dog who tried to pick fights with questions.

"You happy now Jack? This what you wanted with your Uprising? With your Army of Strays?" Other ugly dogs filled in behind him. Torn ears and misaligned jaws filled Jack's vision.

"No," he said. "I'm not happy. I thought we had nothing to lose. I was wrong." A crew of misfits gathered around on Jack's side.

"Oh. You were wrong? You think that's going to get you out of this? You think that's supposed to make everything okay?"

"No," Jack said. He felt tired and mixed up. He wanted this scrap to be settled. "I can't change what's been done. I would if I could, but the past doesn't exist anymore. All we can do is try to stay detached from what's going on right now."

"Detached? What? Like detached from this conversation I'm trying to have with you? Are you saying what I say doesn't matter? Is that what you're saying?"

Later, Jack realized he should have looked down and away. Instead, he looked up and away, giving the ugly Bulldog the impression he was rolling his eyes. Bruno sprang at Jack, and the yard erupted in snarls and snaps as the two groups of inmates tore into each other. Guards ran in with broomsticks and tasers.

Even with the stern warning they received from Administration, the dogs in the Rainbow Building forfeited their rec time privileges again just two days later. Again it was Bruno who lost his cool.

He'd been at a low simmer all day, talking dirt about Jack. "What a rutting idiot. Wasn't it bad enough on the street? Who would listen to some fool old Terrier? Delusional, that's what they were, delusional to think they were going to get away with it. I didn't have nothing to do with no Uprising. No reason I should be walking the Rainbow Bridge because of his gangly ass."

The playground was tense. Scattered pairs and packs spoke quietly, if at all. Even the dogs on the half basketball court played without giving each other dirt. The ball was the loudest sound in the playground: its bounce on the concrete, its thump against the backboard.

The surrounding quiet made the Bulldog seem that much louder.

"Rutting smug bastard. Sitting over there like his dirt don't stink, like he's better than us. I'm gonna give him a piece of my mind."

"Don't, Bruno," said the Pit Lab next to him. "Nothing good can come from it, dog."

"Rut off, beta," Bruno said. He walked, flexing his strong chest and neck muscles, over to where Jack sat with six other dogs. The one closest to Jack was a nervous, skinny Greyhound named Simon, who had taken it upon himself to coordinate Jack's guard, making sure Jack never went anywhere alone.

Bruno started talking while he was still walking up on Jack, "What makes you so special? Huh?"

"Leave him alone," Simon said.

"Can't speak for yourself? Come on, dog. Speak," Bruno taunted Jack.

"He doesn't have to talk to you," Simon said, positioning himself between the ugly Bulldog and the stately Great Dane.

Jack hadn't spoken since his last run-in with Bruno. In his room, he'd been seeing things; he didn't know where he was half the time. Unsure what was real and what wasn't, and not wanting to talk to hallucinations because he thought that might make them stronger, he kept quiet. But this felt real enough.

"It's okay, Simon," he said, startling the Greyhound.

"There he is!" Bruno said. "Fantastic. You gonna answer my question? What makes you so special?"

"I'm not," Jack said.

"So why are we here then?" Bruno opened his arms wide, gesturing at all the dogs in the playground. "Because you're a regular dog? Just an average mutt? We're all going to *die* because of your stupid rutting Uprising for what? No reason?"

"I'm sorry," Jack said, his voice deep and steady. "Is that what you want to hear? I'm sorry so many dogs joined us of their own free will. I'm sorry you expect me to have control over things I can't control. I'm sorry you can't see the bigger picture: that the Uprising did its job. It showed the Norms what it's like to live with the fear of having nothing. I didn't want any of this." He held up a paw and circled it around to indicate the Shelter. "But this is where we are, and a wise dog once told me, 'Happiness is to be of good heart and never distressed, wherever one is and whatever the moment may bring.'"

Jack's speech was more than Bruno could stand. "You pretentious asshole." He snarled and lunged for Jack, but the speedy Greyhound threw himself in the way and received the full force of Bruno's punishing bite. Simon let out a high-pitched yelp as the Bulldog ripped out a chunk of his neck.

Bruno spat Simon's flesh to the ground and backed away. "You rutting idiot. Why'd you get in the way?"

Jack fell to his knees and picked up the Greyhound whose blood was spurting across the grass and onto the concrete of the basketball court.

"Why did you do that?" Jack asked. "It was my fight."

With his dying breath, Simon said, "We're all we've got."

For killing Simon, Bruno was the first dog to be put down at the Shelter. There was no fuss, no ceremony, not even a last meal. He was simply led away and never came back.

14

DESTINY SCHOOLS DIOGENES

"I know who you are," Destiny whispered. Her subconscious had put the pieces together overnight. She hovered over Diogenes, waiting for him to wake up.

Destiny had spent the last few weeks hiding from the police. She got by on her ability to pass as a purebred. Norms were far more likely to help someone they saw as their genetic equal or superior.

"Oh no! I've locked my keys and my wallet in my car! Can you spare just a few dollars so I can pay for this (check/food/water)? I can pay you back as soon as the locksmith gets here. He said thirty to forty-five minutes. What? Really? No, I couldn't. Well, if you're sure. How generous."

The most important thing was staying clean. A believable purebred wouldn't be dirty. So she spent part of what she collected on truck-stop showers, and she did her best to sleep indoors every night. She could usually find an open or jimmy-able door among the warehouses along the highway.

Destiny had come across a few other strays during the last half month. Once they were sure of each other's homelessness, they would talk quickly, exchange news: which Dumpsters were booby-trapped; which, if any, restaurants and supermarkets were setting out-of-date but still edible food to the side for them; where the police were last seen staking out. It was during one of these side-mouth conversations that she learned about the Rainbow Building and what was happening to dogs who ditched their foster families. Dogs like her.

But Destiny didn't have time to think about the future or the past. She was too busy thinking about food and shelter and not getting caught. And on those nights when her stomach was full and she'd found a reasonably hidden and warm place to lay down, she didn't think at all.

Last night had been one of those nights until a small, old dog came into the warehouse where she was sleeping. The noises he made woke her. She heard the rolling garage door—the same one she'd come in—hit the concrete. She heard paws shuffle through the maze of boxes toward the utility room, where she was curled up by the water heater. The door opened and Destiny sprang to her feet.

"You closed the door," he said.

"Who are you?" she asked. The dog looked odd, as if a short-haired Terrier and a wire-haired one had been stuck together lengthwise.

"Never close the door. A closed door is a sign of occupancy."

"Are you a stray?"

"I am not homeless," he said. "The whole world is my home."

Frustrated with her inability to get a straight answer from him, Destiny advanced. Showing her teeth she said, "You cannot snitch on me."

"My good bitch," he said. "I would never."

She relaxed. "Thank you for sparing me. I'm sorry if I'm in your space. I can find somewhere else to sleep."

"Dear Poodle, I'm not *sparing* you. I simply do not believe in the system—not the way it was before, when a stray was able to wander free, to sleep outdoors, to beg on the streets—and not the way it is now. As for where you sleep, it could not matter less to me."

The Terrier turned around three times and lay down, sealing the conversation.

"I know who you are," Destiny said, poking Diogenes in the ribs. She was tired of waiting for him to wake up. She'd had a lot of time to think and she had questions for this little dog.

The Terrier opened his eyes.

"I said, I know who you are."

"That's great," Diogenes said, rubbing his snout with his paws. "Who am I?"

"Where were you?" Destiny asked. "Where did you go when all the homeless dogs were looking for you?"

The story of the Uprising was becoming a legend among the strays. She'd heard it dozens of times, as far back as her first day in the dry riverbed encampment.

Diogenes stood and stretched forward and back. "I was injured."

"That's not a place. Where were you?"

"I was staying with a family I know."

"Why didn't you tell anyone where you were? They thought you were dead. That's what brought the Army of Strays together and set off the Uprising."

"And look where that's gotten us. Idiots!" Diogenes said. He stepped over to the wall and started pissing on it.

Destiny turned away and asked, "Why didn't you go to the park? Why didn't you stop them if they were getting it so wrong?"

Diogenes, done with his morning whiz, stood in the middle of the cramped room. He didn't answer right away. Instead, he sneezed and shook himself from head to toe.

"The family I was staying with lives in the foothills," he said, less boisterous than he'd been a minute ago. "And, as I said, I was injured. I couldn't just traipse along to the park downtown."

Destiny scoffed. "Back up, dog. The foothills? Your ideas are spray-painted everywhere. Didn't you say 'less is better'? 'Extract yourself from the system'? What? That's all well and good until *you* need something?"

"For your information—not that I need to explain myself to you or to anyone else—I was a tutor for this family before I chose to live free. They have always respected me and heeded my advice."

"That makes it okay? *We* should all be self-sufficient but *you* get a safety net?" Destiny wasn't as angry as she was incredulous. "What if it was some other stray who got mauled and needed help, but they'd gotten rid of everything, cut all their ties? How many other homeless dogs have a family in the foothills they can count on?"

"In the end," Diogenes said, "I didn't either. Once my name was attached to this ridiculous Uprising, they turned me out."

"You're a liar."

"I am not. What I've said is what happened."

94

"Not that. You lied to those dogs. You planted seeds of ideas you don't live by. You're a hypocrite. You scorn the very society you rely on for support. Even without your family in the foothills, you live on the system's castoffs. You need the system as much as anyone. Do you know about the Shelter?"

"Of course. Why do you think I'm hiding in here with you and not sleeping out under the stars?"

"Then you know they've already killed one stray and Jack is next?"

For the first time, Diogenes didn't answer.

Destiny went on, "Jack—who listened to you, who led the Army of Strays in your name. They're going to stick a needle in his vein and put him to sleep because of you."

"I didn't force him to do any of what he did. I didn't even ask him to."

"But haven't you read his statement? It was everywhere, everyone read it—Norm or stray. He said it was a simple three-step argument. Step one: if you can see a better way, it's your responsibility to take action. Step two: pockets should be empty—no wallets, no phones. Step three: Therefore, because he knew how to make pockets empty—how to make wallets and phones irrelevant—according to you, Jack had a responsibility to make that happen. He knew it wouldn't be permanent, but it would give the Norms of Black Hill a little taste of the *freedom* that comes from having less. So no, you old cur, you don't get to relinquish yourself. You're culpable. You're responsible. It wouldn't have happened without you, and it wouldn't have happened if you'd been there to stop it."

"Fine," Diogenes said. "They misconstrued my ideas. What do you want me to do?"

"Stop the Shelter from killing any more strays. Stop the Shelter from killing Jack."

15

LIFE ON THE FARM

There were dogs everywhere. Big dogs and little dogs. Black, brown, red, yellow, blue, white, tricolor, brindle, merle, ticked, and speckled dogs. Ears and tails of all shapes and sizes. Easily a hundred dogs. And they were all barking.

The Farm hadn't been easy to find, but Destiny had an ace in her pocket.

"I'm looking for Phyllis," she said whenever she found a stray.

"Don't know nothing about that."

"See this dirty Terrier with me? This is Diogenes. He and I are looking for Phyllis."

"You're supposed to be dead, dog."

"So they tell me."

"I don't know where Phyllis and her Canine Brigade are. But I know somebody who might know."

And on they went across the city, from stray to stray, until they found someone who could tell them what they needed to know, until they stood outside a chained-closed five-bar gate being barked at by a hundred dogs.

"Enough!" a voice snapped at the horde from behind. Quiet spread across the yard from the center out. The glut of dogs near the gate parted, making way for Phyllis and the two beefy Staffordshires who flanked her.

When Phyllis saw Diogenes, she stopped advancing. Her lip curled. "No rutting way," she said.

"We should leave," Diogenes said to Destiny. "Obviously, I am not wanted here."

But Destiny ignored him. "We're here," she said to Phyllis, "because we want to help Jack."

At the name "Jack" the yard erupted in barking all over again. Phyllis and her brace of bodyguards came closer to the gate.

"Quiet!" she threw over her shoulder. She was quickly obeyed. "Let them in."

One of the Staffies unlocked the padlock and whipped the chain off the gate with a reverberating clang. Destiny startled at the noise.

"Come with me," Phyllis said. She led them through the sea of dogs. Destiny kept her eyes on the ground and felt herself trying to shrink. After far too long, they arrived at a large corrugated tin barn, and as they entered it, Destiny felt the intimidation of the crowd begin to ease.

They wove around several vehicle carcasses—old trucks, a couple of cars, and a tractor—and then came to an open space which held some ratty furniture, a dirty area rug, and scattered blankets.

"Please," Phyllis said looking at Destiny, "sit."

Once they were all settled—Phyllis on the ripped-up armchair with the Staffies standing on either side of her, and Destiny and

Diogenes on the couch—Phyllis spoke to Diogenes, "We'd heard rumors, but I really didn't think they were true. You're supposed to be dead, old dog."

"Sorry to disappoint you."

"Someday," she said. "And I do want to hear all about your disappearing act, but before that," she turned her attention to Destiny, "you said something about saving Jack?"

At the name, the Staffordshires' ears perked up and they looked at Phyllis.

"I'm sorry," Destiny said. "I don't mean to be rude, but why does everyone around here react to that name the way they do?"

"These dogs," Phyllis said, "are what is left of the Army of Strays, and in solidarity with our incarcerated leader, we have all taken his name."

"Every dog here is named Jack?" Destiny asked.

"Yes."

"Even you?"

"At heart, but in reality it was far too confusing. Now, you have a plan?" Phyllis looked from Destiny to Diogenes.

"Don't look at me," he said. "None of this was my idea."

"No, of course it wasn't. It has to do with actually helping out another dog."

"That isn't fair, Phyllis," Diogenes said calmly. "I tried to help all of you by teaching you the truth. The problem is that you tried to apply what I said about individual dogs to all dogs. Dogs can change, *one at a time*. Through hard work on themselves, they can discover the truth and live an enlightened life. The same isn't true about society at large. That was your mistake."

"Diogenes," Phyllis said, "I've had a long time to think about this, and I say this in all sincerity: shut the rut up and never talk to me about your selfish, pompous ideas again. If you have something *useful* to say, something that will help us get something *done*, I want to hear it. Otherwise, shut your yap."

Diogenes raised his eyebrows, the one overgrown and the one growing out, and settled back into the couch.

"Now," Phyllis continued, "let's start again. You have a plan to save Jack?" she said to Destiny.

"No, I don't have a plan. I just ran into Diogenes here and couldn't believe he wasn't doing anything to help. I thought I could somehow use him to make something happen."

Phyllis nodded.

Destiny went on. "I'd heard about what you're doing here—taking in strays, keeping dogs safe—and I thought if anybody could make things right it would be you." She found herself looking into the Cattle Dog's eyes as she said this. In Phyllis she saw a dog who was strong but not hard, who had power and wanted to use it for others. She became aware of a budding hope that Phyllis would save *her* from the exhausting void her life had become. Embarrassed at these unspoken thoughts, afraid her need was apparent in her eyes, she looked away, down to the dingy rug.

Phyllis didn't answer right away, and Destiny was glad for the moment to collect herself.

"We've had some ideas about how to save Jack, but none of them seem feasible," Phyllis said. "We'll have a meeting after dinner to discuss our options. You're welcome to attend."

"Dinner?" Destiny asked.

"Let me show you around," Phyllis said to Destiny. "You can come too," she spat at Diogenes.

"If it's all the same to you, this old dog needs some rest." He spread out on the couch.

"Good with me. Let's go," Phyllis said to Destiny.

They left the barn through the back. In the afternoon sun, Destiny was able to take in the vastness of the property.

"How many acres is this place?"

"Ten, I think," Phyllis answered.

"It's not yours?"

"No. It's Dave's. You'll meet him."

The ground was packed earth with weeds edging the fence. Besides the barn, there were three other buildings Destiny could see.

"Let's visit the stables first," Phyllis said, and they walked over to a large wooden structure. At one point, it had been red with white trim, but now it was nearly as brown and thirsty as the ground. Phyllis heaved the rolling door along its squeaky track.

"Hello ladies," she said as they entered. There were eight stalls, four of which were occupied by brood mothers and their whelps. Upon seeing the pups Destiny's eyes lit up and her heart expanded in her chest.

"This is Destiny," Phyllis told them.

"Hello." "Welcome." "Are you pregnant?"

"No," she said, "I'm not. Maybe someday."

"Well," one heavy-lidded momma dog said, "you ever need a puppy fix, I could always use a babysitter."

"Me too," said another.

"Wish you could feed them, too. My teats are killing me. Hey, catch that one!"

Phyllis scooped up the errant whelp and placed it back with its litter.

"I'm just showing Destiny around," Phyllis said, turning to look at the Poodle. "Hopefully she'll be staying with us."

"Wonderful to meet you all," Destiny said, and the two females took a minute to scritch the puppies before they continued the tour.

"Come. I want to show you the shed."

They trotted across the yard to an outbuilding that was far newer and better maintained than the stables. Cables ran from the eaves of a nearby trailer to the top of the shed and disappeared inside it.

"Why aren't the mothers and babies in here?" Destiny asked.

"For one thing, they wouldn't fit. And for another . . . you'll see."

Phyllis slid open the well-oiled shed door, saying "As you were," to the Jacks inside. The shed was a bright and busy place full of desks and chairs; bulky, mismatched computers; printers and shredders; and dogs clacking at keyboards, shuffling paper, and waiting on machines.

"This is where we create 'fosters' to get dogs out of the Shelter."

"Identity theft?" Destiny asked.

"More like identity fabrication," Phyllis said. She turned to an Australian Shepherd with facial markings that made it look like he wore glasses. "How many so far, Jack?"

"Thirty saved. Should be thirty-two by the end of the week."

"That's fantastic," Destiny said.

"Unemployed tech workers are a dangerous thing," Phyllis said smiling. "All right, let's go meet Dave."

They climbed the wooden steps to the house, a double wide on cinder blocks. Phyllis knocked on the door.

"Just a minute," a rough voice called out.

"We won't be going in," Phyllis said to Destiny. "Dave collects more than dogs."

"Oh," Destiny said, the realization dawning. "He's a hoarder," she whispered.

Quickly and quietly, as the doorknob turned from the inside, Phyllis hushed her, "We don't use that word." And then, "Hi Dave," she said, returning to her regular voice.

An old Basset Hound with a white blind eye stood in the doorway leaning on a cane. He turned aside as a cough ruffled his pendulous jowls, and Destiny could see thick vertebrae protruding from his hunched back.

"This is Destiny. Just wanted to introduce you."

"Destiny? Don't you mean Jack?" He said it as if it were a little joke of theirs.

"She isn't sure if she's staying yet."

While they were talking, Destiny was trying to see inside, but all she could make out were stacks of *National Geographic* magazines and wire crates full of tennis balls.

"Well, you're welcome here little miss," Dave said. "Not that Phyllis needs any more help getting into trouble." He winked his live eye.

"Thank you," Destiny said.

"See you for dinner?" Phyllis asked the old dog.

"Yes. Today I think I'll make it."

Dave went back inside and the females headed back to the barn.

"Is he unwell?" Destiny asked.

"He's rutting crazy, if that's what you mean. Got a savior complex. Thinks we're all his children. He used to let a couple strays sleep in the barns, and when the Shelter opened he sent them out to gather up as many homeless as they could. We got wind of it and came to see if we could use the place for our purposes. He thinks what we do is some kind of game."

"Seems like he means well enough, and it does work in your favor," Destiny said. "But that cough, the cane, not making it to dinner—he's sick, isn't he?"

"Oh, yes. Distemper. Never got his shots."

"Damn."

They were back at the barn. Phyllis opened the door for Destiny.

"Yeah," she said. "It's hard to watch. He probably only has a few months left."

The females entered the building to find Diogenes standing in the middle of a throng of Jacks.

"And that is why," he expounded, "even with the best of intentions, everything touched by dogs becomes tainted and corrupt."

"No!" Phyllis barked. "No you don't." She grabbed him by his scruff and yanked him away from the circle. "Get the door," she said to Destiny.

Destiny watched from the doorway as Phyllis hauled Diogenes to the stables and threw him in with the brood mothers.

"Make sure he stays here until I come for him," she heard Phyllis command her Staffordshires.

When she got back to the barn, the two females shared a smile. Diogenes would either pass a quiet couple of hours or he'd be in for it.

Later that evening, after a soup-kitchen-style dinner, Phyllis retrieved a subdued Diogenes from the stables and called the higher-ranking Jacks together in the barn.

"You all know why we're here," she said to her troops. "To come up with a plan to save Jack."

Many of the Jacks clapped or yipped or huffed at this.

"And you know that we've had this meeting before, many times, without coming up with a workable solution, and that every time a new dog comes to the Farm, we have this meeting again. Tonight the potential new Jacks are Destiny," who she indicated with her right paw, "and Diogenes," who she indicated with her left.

The Jacks murmured questions to one another.

"Yes, *that* Diogenes. Let's begin. Does anyone have new ideas about how to save Jack?"

"Go there and take him," one of the Jacks barked out.

"She said she wanted *new* ideas," another Jack said.

"The Rainbow Building is guarded twenty-four seven. We can't just waltz in there," said another.

"Blow it up!"

"Burn it down!"

"Are there any ideas that wouldn't result in more deaths and incarceration?" Phyllis asked.

"Can we change the law?" Destiny offered. "We still live in a democracy, right?"

"The law can be changed," Phyllis said. "But to do that, we'd have to get enough Norms to sign a petition, then it would go on the ballot in November. Jack could die any day now. Plus, we're all strays. We don't have *any* rights, let alone the right to submit a petition to change an ordinance."

"Oh," Destiny said quietly. "Well then," she went on, regaining her confidence, "we could go to the Dog Catcher. He's in charge of the Shelter, and he seems like a decent enough dog."

"Go to him and what?" Diogenes scoffed, speaking up for the first time.

"Ask him not to kill Jack. Appeal to his sense of morality." The Jacks were jeering and shaking their heads. "And if that doesn't work," Destiny went on, speaking over the hubbub, "we threaten the dirt out of him until he frees Jack and disables the euthanasia apparatus."

The crowd quieted down. All eyes turned to Phyllis.

"Can't hurt to try," she said.

Destiny came trotting back across the immense yard after availing herself of one of the pit toilets, which was not as bad as she thought it was going to be.

Small groups of Jacks sat and lay around campfires. She saw Diogenes reclining near one. He looked content, happy to be sleeping under the stars again.

Near another fire, one she was closer to, two Jacks sparred. They growled and threw punches, fangs glistening in the fire light. Destiny didn't know if it was a serious fight or some kind of training. The surrounding Jacks watched with interest but not concern. Either way, Destiny felt herself contract and speed up, practically running for the barn.

"What happened?" Phyllis asked the harried Poodle.

"Nothing," she said. "I'm so embarrassed. It was just a dogfight. It had nothing to do with me."

Jacks were bedding down all over the barn.

"Come with me," Phyllis said, picking up a blanket and shaking it out. She led Destiny to one of the junker trucks and lowered the tailgate with an ear-piercing squeal. There were long sheets of cardboard and an old backpack in the bed of the truck.

"This is where I sleep. No one will bother you here. You'll be safe."

Destiny's eyes grew wet with tears.

Phyllis said, "It's been a long time since anyone's been kind to you, hasn't it?"

"Will you sleep here too?" Destiny asked.

"If that's what you want."

The two dogs climbed into the truck bed. Destiny began to lie down and Phyllis put the backpack under her head as a pillow. The space was small, and the dogs curled up together.

"Is this ok?" Phyllis asked.

But Destiny couldn't answer. Phyllis' touch had broken her down. Tears flowed freely, and soon her body was racked with sobs. Eventually, Destiny slept from sheer exhaustion. In the morning she felt more rested than she had in months. Maybe years.

16

DOGNAPPING THE DOG CATCHER

Destiny looked like a different dog. She had to if she was going to go anywhere near the Shelter. The last thing the group needed was to have someone recognize an AWOL recidivist among them. So she dyed her hair a rich chestnut brown. No one would know. Only teenagers and old bitches colored their fur.

She liked not being white. She felt as if she attracted less attention.

It was half an hour before the Shelter was supposed to close for the evening when they pulled up to the gate and handed over the identification that proved they were Norms. There were four of them: Destiny, Phyllis, and two Jacks who could pass for purebred as long as they didn't open their yaps—one was a Mastiff and the other a Doberman.

Phyllis parked the old beater they borrowed from Dave as far away from the Administration Building as she could. None of them spoke as they walked toward the former kindergarten. They didn't need to. They knew the plan.

The Administration Building, Destiny noticed, had a fresh coat of tan paint. She was sad to see the playing puppies had been covered up. Inside it still felt like a school. The walls were plastered with "Character Counts!" posters touting values like "fairness" and "caring." The front counter was low and divided reception from a middle area with a couple of desks and filing cabinets. Doors led off the center into private offices. The one at the back said "Dog Catcher" on its opaque window.

"Hello?" Destiny said in the most condescending voice she could muster. "Hello, we'd like some service please?"

It had to be Destiny; she had the look they needed. There was no such thing as a purebred blonde Cattle Dog; that combination was just another mutt. And while there was no rule against mixed breeds fostering strays, Destiny's looks would grease the wheel.

A young Collie emerged from a side office. "Yes ma'am," she said. "How can I help you?"

On two lines, her tag read "Jessica" and "Volunteer."

"I need to see the Dog Catcher."

"Do you have an appointment?"

"You don't understand. *These dogs*," she soaked the words with disdain, "have apparently been promised the same stray as Roger and I."

"If you'll tell me your names, I'm sure we can get it cleared up."

Destiny was hitting her stride now, channeling Mrs. Covington. "No! No, that will not do at all! I *demand* to see the Dog Catcher. He's a public servant, isn't he? Well it is time for him to face the public." By now she was nearly yelling.

"I'm sure we can—" the browbeaten volunteer started to say when a deep, friendly voice called out from the Dog Catcher's office.

"Don't worry about it, Jessica. Just show them in."

Jessica didn't have to do anything. Destiny trotted around the desk with her nose in the air, and the other three followed her into the office. As soon as the four strays were in the little room, Phyllis closed the door.

The big Jacks flanked the Dog Catcher, who continued to eat a banana.

"It's Abe, right?" Destiny said, recalling the name from her brief time in the Green Building.

"That's me. Please excuse the banana," he said throwing the already browning peel in the trash. "Doctor's orders. Potassium's supposed to help with the kidney stones. Can't stand them personally—bananas that is. Stones either for that matter."

"Abe," Phyllis said, "we're going to need you to let Jack go."

The Jacks leaned in closer.

"Ha! That's a good one!"

"We're serious, Abe," Phyllis said.

"I can't do that."

"Sure you can. Aren't you the guy in charge, the Big Kahuna around here, Mr. Dog Catcher?"

"You couldn't be more wrong," he said. "I don't have any power here. I don't have any power anywhere."

"But you do have the keys," Destiny said.

"Yeah, but I can't do it. There are guards and cameras. If I even looked like I was *thinking* about doing anything out of line, I'd be dirt-canned and they'd bring in some other lily-livered beta."

"Who's they, Abe? Who's really in charge around here?" Phyllis asked.

"The city," he answered. "The Council. Sasha."

"Sasha?" Destiny asked.

"Sasha Cavalier. She's president of the Council. This whole thing," he circled a paw in the air, "this is all her."

Phyllis and Destiny checked in with each other.

"We can't leave him here. He could rat us out," Destiny said.

Abe protested. "No! No, I would never. I get it. I'm cool. I used to be in a band."

"She's right," Phyllis said. "You're coming with us."

17

JACK FIGURES SOME DIRT OUT

Jack didn't know when his kill date was; he only knew that it was soon, and that the long days alone with his misfiring mind had left him grasping at the tail end of his sanity.

What would Diogenes say? he asked himself over and over, afraid he was disappointing the memory of his mentor by growing soft under hard circumstances. He lay on his thin mattress, staring at the ceiling, trying to remember.

"Seek out hardships," Diogenes had said, "to thicken your skin."

"Discipline yourself to endure pain and suffering."

"The world is like one of those travel centers off the highway, with a convenience store and a restaurant and an electronics department and oversized stuffed animals. The smart traveler buys only what they need for the journey. To be self-sufficient, we have to abandon the socially created need for things and relationships."

Jack was failing. He missed being around other dogs. He missed his friends. He grieved the future he could have had with them.

"Use adversity to develop indifference, and use that indifference to cope with any situation, whether it's brought about by chance or by the actions of others."

Jack was failing here, too. He wasn't growing *more* resilient, but less. His mind was fragile. His attention pinballed from thought to thought, time to time, place to place. He couldn't control it. His past *was* his present as often as not.

He wondered if his situation was "brought about by chance," or "by the actions of others." There were arguments for both. He hadn't sought out the position of leader of the Army of Strays. Phyllis had laid that mantle on him. But he had been there to take it. Was that chance or the action of another? Where did decisions come into play in Diogenes' philosophy, besides the decision to be indifferent?

What if the world isn't something that happens to you, something you have to duck and weave to avoid? Jack took stock of the decisions he'd made that led him to the Shelter.

He decided to join the military.

He decided to serve one term and get out.

He didn't decide to have PTSD or be unemployable when he got back. He didn't decide to be homeless.

He decided to listen to Diogenes.

He decided to bring dogs together around what Diogenes was saying.

He decided to call attention to Diogenes' disappearance. He could have let it go, but he didn't.

When Phyllis wanted to take action, he could have walked away, but he decided to participate. When Phyllis gave him the role of leader, it had been his choice to take it on. He thought he was doing what was right, even without Diogenes' ideas. If there was a way to give the homeless a voice, even if it was only for a week or a day or an hour, it was worth doing. If it could lead to Norms having an ounce more compassion toward strays, it was worth doing.

So maybe Jack wasn't living up to Diogenes' standards, but maybe Diogenes' standards weren't everything Jack thought they were. Maybe Jack had his own standards, and maybe Jack met those standards just fine.

18

SASHA CAVALIER, PUREBRED BITCH

The house was made of triangles and glass. It was impossible to tell how big it was from the outside; the architecture appeared to fold space-time.

Destiny went to the front door. She'd never been this far up into the foothills. She was nervous, but Phyllis and the two beefy Staffordshires were concealed around the corner. She pressed the buzzer.

A petite Spaniel in a dressing robe and matching slippers opened the door.

"Sasha Cavalier?" Destiny asked as the other three strays bolted through the door and forced their way inside.

"Who are you? What is this?" Sasha's eye were wide, her paws gripped the doorframe.

The invaders' momentum pressed her back into the foyer, and the last Jack closed the door.

"Sasha," Phyllis said. "We need to talk."

"Okay. Sure," Sasha said slowly. "What do you want to talk about?"

"Pretty calm, aren't you Sasha?" Phyllis said.

The Spaniel's eyes flickered toward the door.

"She called the cops," Destiny said, and she pointed to a number pad on the wall and a camera high up in the corner.

"Guess it's the hard way," Phyllis said. "Bag her up, please," she said to the Jacks.

The two big dogs easily restrained the protesting Spaniel.

"I hate yippers," Phyllis said.

The Staffordshires each took Sasha by an arm, lifting her from her feet. She kicked the air from her front door to the trunk of the car.

Sasha was tied to a chair in the barn. Destiny, Phyllis, and dozens of Jacks surrounded her, including the Mastiff and the Doberman as well as the two bull-necked Staffordshires. Phyllis snapped the hood from Sasha's head, revealing a flurry of brown and white fur and a makeshift handkerchief gag, which Phyllis removed.

"What is this?" Sasha said in the tone of a CEO who'd been handed an unfavorable status update.

"A reckoning?" Phyllis said. "Or a discussion. We're going to give you an opportunity to work with us."

"Work with you? With strays? With criminals? I would never."

Phyllis paused a beat, apparently considering what the bitch said.

"Come on now, Sasha. I mean first of all you're not really in a position to resist, and second, you haven't even heard what we're asking."

The Spaniel said nothing and steadfastly avoided eye contact with any of the dogs surrounding her, without looking down.

"All we want is for you not to kill Jack or any of the other strays. They don't die, you don't die."

"Not my call," Sasha said. "You're barking up the wrong tree."

The Jacks grumbled. Phyllis gave them a look that said "Not yet." To Sasha she said, "We heard you were the alpha over there, that everything having to do with the Shelter goes through you."

"I oversee operations, but I oversee the whole city."

Destiny broke into the discussion. Her tone was more placating than Phyllis'. "Come on now. The Shelter's your baby, isn't it? You're proud of it."

"Honestly?" Sasha said, still at their mercy with her paws tied behind her back, her legs fastened to the chair legs. "The Uprising was a godsend. The good dogs of Black Hill deserve to live unmolested by the homeless blight."

"Blight?" Destiny asked.

"You heard me."

The Jacks were at a low rumble now, lips twitching and fangs bared. Sasha Cavalier embodied everything these dogs had come to hate and fear about the Norms.

She went on. "The ordinance for the Shelter passed unanimously. You're parasites. You're ticks on the back of society."

The Jacks were at a boil. A few lunged, only to be held back by those around them.

"Wait!" Phyllis said to them. She turned back to Sasha. "I am the only thing standing between you and this angry pack of strays.

My plan was to threaten you with worms, which half of the dogs here would be happy to share with you."

Sasha's face curled in disgust.

"But they have something far worse in mind. I suggest you work with us."

"Even if I wanted to, I couldn't change anything."

"That can't be true, Sasha," Destiny said, stepping back in. "You have power. You could rescind the ordinance. The Council members will do whatever you tell them too, won't they?"

"That might be true," Sasha said, "but there wouldn't be time to save your Great Dane."

Destiny caught Phyllis's eye. "I'm going to step outside," she said.

Phyllis, lips tight, nodded once.

Sasha could sense that something had been decided, something very bad for her.

"I'm sorry we couldn't come to an agreement," Destiny said to the Spaniel as she walked toward the door.

"Wait!" Sasha said, losing her cool for the first time. "Maybe there is something I can do."

"No," Destiny said turning back. "You're of no use to us. You've made that clear."

"Fine!" Sasha yelled at the room full of strays, "Do your worst, you filthy mongrels. It won't change a thing. *No one wants you.* You had a choice: get with the program or get put down. Just stay off our streets. No one wants to see you, or hear you, or smell you. You're a nuisance to upstanding citizens who work for a living."

Destiny had made her way back to Phyllis' side. They both spread their arms to hold back the Jacks, who were pressing in. It was symbolic, but it worked.

"Enough!" Phyllis commanded the angry dogs. Then she pointed to the Staffordshires. "You two, take her to the stables."

19

THE RESCUE

Abe sat on the tattered couch. Destiny was on his right and Phyllis, with her Staffordshires, was in the armchair to his left.

"You understand what we need you to do?" Phyllis asked.

"Sure do," Abe said, always the gregarious Labrador.

"Some of our purebred-looking Jacks will be with you the whole time, just to make sure."

"You can count on me."

Phyllis turned away from the couch and whistled loud and high. Within seconds a team of four Pit mixes appeared.

"Yes ma'am?" asked the lead dog.

"Prepare for Operation Liberation. We strike at fifteen-hundred hours."

"Yes ma'am," the lead dog said.

What happened next was a flurry of activity. Every Jack had a job and got straight to it.

"What's Operation Liberation?" Destiny asked.

"The fallback plan. Sasha said Jack couldn't wait for a Council meeting. That means we need to get him out of there now. We couldn't use Operation Liberation before because it would have meant dead dogs, but having Abe here makes the plan a whole lot less violent and a whole lot more likely to succeed. I'll show you," Phyllis said. She indicated with her paw for the Staffordshires to keep watch over the Dog Catcher, even though he looked perfectly content to stay right there on the couch.

Destiny went with Phyllis to one of the pickup trucks, which now had its hood raised and three dogs up to their elbows in its engine bay. The females went to the truck bed. Phyllis flung aside the tarp that covered the back and revealed a large and careless pile of guns.

"Another thing Dave collects."

Diogenes went past them rolling a barrel. He soon reached a dead end and rolled the barrel back again.

"Why are you doing that?" Destiny asked as he passed by.

"To look as busy as the rest of you. What are you doing?"

"We're going to save Jack."

"Then what are you going to do, after you save him? Replace one flawed system with another?"

Destiny turned toward Phyllis, looking for an answer.

"I don't know what will happen then," Phyllis said. "I only know that this is what we have to do now."

Abe and the two Jacks entered the Administration Building first, followed closely by Destiny and Phyllis. The females stayed in front of the receiving desk while Abe led the Jacks right past it.

"Jessica, these dogs are here from the city for a surprise inspection."

"It's Veronica, sir," the Sheepdog working the desk said.

"Right. Sorry, Veronica. Please tell the guards I want to see them in the conference room at shift change for a short meeting. Both shifts, coming and going."

"Yes sir," Veronica said picking up the phone. Abe and the two Jacks went into his office and closed the door.

Destiny and Phyllis waited until the Sheepdog—whose corded locks were interwoven with crystals and feathers—hung up the phone before they approached and turned themselves in as strays.

Veronica took them to the gym and led them through their in-processing, where they were scrubbed clean and given blue pants and white t-shirts. They were assigned to the Violet Building, and the Sheepdog led them to their bunks at the far end of the radiating hall.

"We're almost at capacity," Veronica said. "You're lucky to be getting beds."

"What happens when there isn't any more room?" Destiny asked.

The hippie dog looked confused for a long minute as her mind sizzled with cognitive dissonance. She worked at the Shelter because she wanted to help the homeless, but she also knew the Shelter was going to put down dogs who couldn't be placed. Her eyes glazed over.

"Hello?" Destiny waved her paw in front of Veronica's snout. "I said, what happens when there isn't any more room?"

"I'm sure we'll just move some things around," Veronica said, dismissing the topic. "Dinner is served for the Violet Building at 7:30. If you need anything else, I'm sure one of your bunkmates can help you out."

The minute Veronica was out of sight, Destiny took Phyllis to the Green Building.

As they trotted down the green and white tiled hallway, she said, "They're probably gone, but I know they'll help us if they're still here."

Destiny opened the door to the room she was assigned to her first time in the Shelter.

"Ruby! You're still here!"

"Of course I am, beauty queen. Nobody's dumb enough to foster a stubborn old bitch like me."

Destiny saw her point. The sleek, black dog was imposingly regal, and as soon as she opened her mouth it was clear she wasn't taking orders from anyone. Ruby never had a chance in the Shelter.

"Ruby, this is Phyllis."

"*The* Phyllis?" Ruby asked the Cattle Dog.

"The only Phyllis I know," the Cattle Dog said back.

"What's going on?" Ruby asked. "If the stories are true, there's no way you'd end up here accidentally."

"We're getting everyone out," Destiny said. "Are Belle and Beau and Peter still here?"

"Funny thing how two Pariahs and an old man seem to have been overlooked by the good folks of Black Hill all this time," Ruby said, iron-plating her words with sarcasm.

"Good," Destiny said. "They can help let everybody know."

Word spread quickly from room to room, dog to dog. "Be ready. Something big is going down when the Rainbow Building guards change shifts."

Destiny saw a few business casual employees talking animatedly to each other, and a few volunteers with glassy looks like the one Veronica had. She knew someone would go to the Dog Catcher and warn him that something was up with the strays, and that Abe would reassure them that everything was fine.

The Shelter buzzed with anticipation. And while they couldn't warn the dogs inside the Rainbow Building, Destiny believed they knew. The air crackled with energy. They had to feel it.

As 3 p.m. neared, the new guards started showing up at the Administration Building in fresh uniforms, ready for the swing shift, and the guards getting off duty showed up at the building rumpled and ready to go home. Destiny couldn't see what was happening in there. She could only hope things were going according to plan. She visualized the dogs filing into the conference room, and Abe starting his painfully boring presentation while one of the Jacks locked the door. She pictured him slogging through his slides of statistics and projections.

While she couldn't see that, what she could see were Dave's beat-up old trucks pulling up to the gate. They were loaded down with Jacks, every third one armed with some kind of gun.

The gate guard, one of only a few not in the meeting with Abe, was yelling out of the guard shack window while one of the trucks backed up and then rammed the barrier out of commission. The gate's frame bent and the whole thing swung open, with the chainlink hanging like loose metal drapes. The trucks drove into the school parking lot, lining up in the drop-off and pick-up zone.

Six armed Jacks approached the gate guard, who had drawn his gun. The lead Jack said something—they were too far away for Destiny to hear—and the guard dog ran off the property and down the neighborhood road.

This first wave of Jacks trotted, almost in time with each other, into the Administration Building. It was important to keep the guards out of the way.

Destiny watched as a business casual here, a volunteer there went for their phones, but nearby strays plucked them from their paws. "You should leave now," Destiny heard one of them say. "And you probably don't want to be the one who calls this in. That's a matter of public record, you know." Soon there was no one around but the strays.

The second wave of Jacks arrived by the carload and spread out through the campus. Every few minutes Destiny heard a BANG or a POP-POP and knew one of theirs had run into a guard as they went about their work of flushing out the Shelter dogs. She could only hope they were okay.

From near and far, Destiny heard Jacks yelling: "If you can run, run. If you can't run, get to a truck." Strays scrambled in all directions. Jacks carried the disabled and the elderly to the parking lot.

The contingent of four Pit mixes marched up to Phyllis.

"Ma'am," their leader said.

"Let's get to it," she said back.

The six dog pack—Destiny, Phyllis, and the four Pit Bulls—skulked their way from building to building while the pandemonium around them increased. A nearby gunshot startled Destiny and she froze.

"No time for that now," Phyllis said, dragging the Poodle along by the scruff until she could get her paws back under her.

When they got to the Rainbow Building, the Pits used crowbars and sledgehammers on the reinforced door. It fell toward them into the dirt, and a cloud of dust rose up and hung heavy in the air.

"Behind me," Phyllis said, holding her gun out in front of her.

As the dust settled it revealed the form of a guard—a German Shepherd. He stood in the hallway a few doors down from the entrance with his sidearm drawn and leveled. He was panting, as if he'd been racing for the door. Tension enveloped the pack like a thunderstorm.

Destiny's adrenaline, which she thought was at maximum, spiked even further. The guard was a purebred, a perfect twin of her abusive husband. She felt her heart drop pounding into her stomach. She felt her will shrivel inside her. In the time between two blinks, the long central hallway of the Rainbow Building disappeared and she was back in the marble and glass bathroom, curled up—hopeless and suicidal—on the expensive, scratchy bathmat.

Tears flooded her eyes.

"No," she whispered. "That isn't who I am anymore."

Taking a step forward into the no-dog's-land between her group and the guard, Destiny wiped the tears from her eyes. Phyllis reached out, grabbed her arm, but Destiny shrugged her off. "I'm just a Poodle," she said, looking at the guard. "What harm could I possibly do?" She took another step forward, maybe four more steps to go.

Bang! Bang! Bang! surprised them all. Not guns this time, but death row dogs, hearing what was happening in the hallway, hitting their doors with anything that would make noise.

"Louder!" Phyllis yelled.

Her command ramped up the guard's panic, and he moved the gun off of the Poodle and onto the Cattle Dog. Destiny lunged the remaining distance. The gun fired as she wrapped her jaw around the German Shepherd's paw.

Out of the corner of her eye, Destiny saw Phyllis fall. She pried her teeth from the yowling dog's flesh, and the gun clattered to the floor. She picked it up.

"Stay," she said to the spitting image of her ex as she stepped behind him. He stood still, paws raised, including the one dripping blood from torn patches of fur and skin. Destiny squared herself behind the guard's left leg and, using the adrenaline flooding her veins and all the strength in her hindquarters, she kicked him. With a loud crack, the guard's femur detached from its hip socket. A genetic weakness of Shepherds, it was something she'd dreamt of doing to her husband hundreds of times. To have carried it out was satisfying, even if it wasn't on the right dog.

The guard crumpled to the floor.

Destiny ran to where Phyllis lay sprawled on the tile. She'd been shot through the thigh and the floor all around her was slick with blood. Two of the Pits were tightening a tourniquet.

"Stop looking at me like that," Phyllis said to Destiny. "We have a job to do." One of the Pits hefted Phyllis up and supported her while she stood. "Let's get to work."

The Pit Bulls used their brawn to break into one classroom after another. "Go, go, go," they said as each door opened and they ushered the chronically homeless toward another chance at life. When they got to the last room, to Jack's room, he was at the door, trying to hear what he could through the small window. Phyllis tore the paper away from the glass and tears sprang to Jack's eyes when he saw her.

"Stand back!" She had to shout to be heard through the door and over the increasing din. Inside the Rainbow Building and out, strays were everywhere, yelling to each other, finding loved ones from whom they didn't want to be separated, and running for freedom.

Phyllis motioned to the Pit Bull helping her stand and they moved out of the way. The others went to work.

When the door was open, Jack dashed out to Phyllis.

"You're hurt," he said. "We need to get you to a vet."

Phyllis turned to the leader of the Pits. "Stick to the plan. Empty the Admin Building, then send out the sweepers. When a building is clear, break the windows and douse it with kerosene. Move fast, the cops must be on their way by now."

20

JACK AND DIOGENES MAKE TRACKS

It had been 24 hours since the Army of Strays made their mad dash away from the burning school—many on paw because the cars and trucks were full of civilians—but the police still hadn't shown up at the Farm. Maybe no one had been caught. Maybe they'd been caught but didn't squeal. Or maybe the cops were on their way. If that was the case, they were in for a standoff.

Jack, Diogenes, Destiny, and Phyllis sat on the ratty barn furniture. Phyllis had her bandaged leg propped up on a crate. It would be a few days before they knew the extent of the damage caused by both the bullet and the tourniquet. The dogs had stayed up late talking, catching Jack up on everything he'd missed, and then they spent a sleepless night waiting for the sound of sirens and listening as strays crept into the crowded barn after their long and dangerous treks back from Operation Liberation.

"I wish we could have watched it burn," Phyllis said. The others laughed their agreement.

Surprising himself Jack said, "Stig should be here." The statement provoked a moment of silence, and a recognition in Jack that he was done burying his pain. Wherever that well had been, his time in the Shelter had sealed it.

"When do you leave?" Phyllis asked.

"Sundown," Jack said. "Wish I didn't have to. I really like what you've got going on here."

"I don't," Diogenes said. "I'm coming with you."

Jack didn't object. He might not have been enamored with everything Diogenes had to say, but he still considered him a friend.

The little Terrier and the towering Great Dane left after dinner. Dave gave them one of the old trucks, and the Jacks, who had all reverted to their given names, gave them new identities and took up a collection for gas money.

Destiny and Phyllis waved goodbye from the five-bar gate.

CODA: SIX MONTHS LATER

They looked different now. Destiny was white again, and Phyllis was three-legged, managing well with crutches.

"Heard from Jack," Phyllis said to Destiny as she sat down at the kitchen table with their morning coffee.

In the months after the fire at the Shelter, Dave had protected his dogs (including all of his new ones). He gave them addresses and alibis and time to dispose of any incriminating evidence when he insisted the police have a warrant when they showed up at the five-bar gate. There had been so many dogs there that day, none of the witnesses could point to any one dog and say whether they'd been a Shelter dog or with the Army of Strays. Eventually, the cops were forced to back off, leaving the Farm with an empty threat: "We're keeping an eye on you."

And when Dave went over the Rainbow Bridge shortly after that, he left Phyllis the Farm on the condition that she keep it open to strays. After months of work, she and Destiny had reclaimed the trailer from his heaving collections of magazines and tennis balls, paperwork, coffee mugs, and computer parts from the 1990s.

"What'd Jack have to say?" Destiny asked.

"He got a job. Security guard at a factory. Lots of time to himself."

"That's great," Destiny said. "Any word about Diogenes?"

"He is in the wind."

"And I'm sure that suits him just fine."

"You about ready?" Phyllis asked.

Destiny took a final swig of her coffee and the two of them headed out to the yard for breakfast with the troops. When they were done, they went to the mess, same as they did every day, and loaded a cart with plates of food for the brood mothers. Since Operation Liberation, the stables (like the rest of the Farm) had been nearly full.

Destiny pushed the cart and Phyllis swung herself ahead and shouldered open the stubborn door. They were greeted with the squeals and whimpers of newborn pups and the smiles and Oh-thank-God-I'm-starvings of the mamas.

Destiny took one plate deep into the building, past all the mothers and babies, back where the light barely reached. And there in the last stall lay a creature who might have once been brown and white, but who was now so covered with dirt and grime that her fur was matted and hay stuck to her in clumps.

"Morning meal, Sasha," Destiny announced, banging on the wall to rouse her.

She placed the plate on the ground at the end of the chained dog's reach. Sasha looked up. Her left eye twitched.

"Who knows," Destiny said, "maybe you'll get some time in the yard today."

Amy M. Vaughn is the author of *Freak Night at the Slee-Z Motel* and *Skull Nuggets* and editor of the bizarro writing prompt collection *Dog Doors to Outer Space*. She lives in Tucson, Arizona, in her little house with her little family, which includes a few not so little rescues.